GRAVESIDE GAMBLER

A RILEY CRUZ NOVEL: BOOK FIVE

L.A. McBRIDE

FOREWORD

This series takes place in the same world as the Kali James series. Each series can be read independently. Although every effort has been made to avoid major spoilers, the events in this book overlap with those of Kali's series and include some shared details.

CHAPTER 1

*L*ife as a thief taught me a myriad of ways I could go out—a job gone sideways, a vengeful mark, even something as mundane as a faulty garage door. Wrestling a full-grown Mojave rattlesnake hadn't made the list. Fortunately, my reflexes were quick enough to catch him mid-strike. There were only two things I could think to do with the rattler I now had by the neck. Since it wasn't his fault I'd practically landed on him, killing him was out of the question. That left me belting out the lyrics to "Shake It Off" in a desperate attempt to charm him.

"For fuck's sake, this is not the time for karaoke, Riley." Nash peered over the edge of the mesa above me.

When Nash's boot had hit crumbling rock a few minutes ago, I'd barely had enough time to shove him to safety before the rockslide sent me careening down the cliff. The Alatyr stone talisman he wore might make him virtually invincible, but crashing down the side of a cliff would still hurt. Besides, I could shift into a goat and climb up far faster than he could, so I hadn't been too worried. At least, not until the telltale rattling.

I ignored Nash and kept singing. From the irritated rattle smacking my belly, serenading the snake wasn't working out the way I'd hoped.

"You're not gonna kill that snake, are you?" Nash sounded resigned.

"Nope." If there was one thing I understood on a bone-deep level, it was the instinct to fight when cornered. I gave up on the singing and tried to mimic the snake's hissing. Maybe if I attempted to bond with him in his native tongue, he'd cut me some slack.

The rattling got louder, those slitted eyes fixed on my throat.

"Work with me here, buddy," I muttered. I hadn't survived twenty-five years without becoming a vamp snack to allow this guy to get in a strike. But we were at a draw.

Nash let out an exaggerated sigh. "Then toss him down the cliff."

I tilted my head to stare up at him, making sure I kept a firm grip on the snake. "I can't do that. He's already scared."

After one last disgusted look at me, Nash stalked off, marveling out loud I'd survived this long. A few minutes later, he returned with an empty backpack that had a rope looped through the straps. Instead of tossing it over the side, he lowered it down to me. "Put him inside," Nash said. "I'll haul him up and dump him on the big rock we sat on."

"Promise you'll be gentle?"

Nash shook the rope. "I promise not to hurt the venomous snake. Now will you stick him in the backpack already, so you can shift, and we can get out of this blasted desert?" The Chihuahuan Desert didn't agree with Nash. Within an hour of our hike, his face had been flushed from the sun, his attitude even surlier than usual.

I reached for the bag with one hand while holding the snake away from my body with my other hand. I should've known it'd come down to a standoff with a viper. My mother had baked the warning right into the tale.

The problem with my mom's bedtime stories was that she'd made the treacherous terrain and death-defying odds sound like a grand adventure. Staring into the eyes of an angry rattlesnake as I stuffed him into a knapsack qualified more as a stupid way to die than a fun adventure, though.

A few weeks ago, when Kage Sato read my mother's will, a real-life scavenger hunt seemed fun. After taking a knife to the gut and busting Martha Matthew's blood rune operation in Kansas City, chasing down the clues to find a demon arti-fact my mother hid decades ago was a welcome break. But after a couple days camping in the desert while attempting to recreate one of Mel's dream adventures, I was starting to think this might not be as easy as she'd made it sound.

Her first clue had been, "Find your guide in the stories, solace in your memories, and courage in your marrow." That last bit should've tipped me off. Instead, I'd focused on the memories and the stories.

I'd recalled over two dozen bedtime stories in varying degrees of detail. While recovering from my stab wound, I recorded every story, doing my best not to jumble them together, but a child's memory had a lot of holes. Dez and I had sifted through the recordings to narrow it down to three contenders—each with a setting matching New Mexico, where I had grown up.

The great Chihuahuan Desert race story that landed me here was number two. First, we'd spent several days bumming around in Roswell. Admittedly, that adventure had been more fun. It had also been a big, fat bust. At least there, I'd scored a set of shot glasses with alien-eyed chili peppers. They were going to look epic on my new bar shelving at headquarters. The only souvenir I was likely to get from today's adventure was a snake bite.

Once I had the rattlesnake safely zipped into the backpack, I peeled off my boots and hiking pants.

"Woah." Nash covered his eyes like the midday sun was blinding. Of course, he wasn't looking at the sun. "Warn a guy before you get naked."

I rolled my eyes. For a man who spent a decade as a Green Beret, Nash sure had delicate sensibilities. When I finished stripping, I stuffed everything into the backpack's second compartment and tugged on the rope. "All set," I hollered up.

While Nash rehomed my new friend, I shifted into my goat and spent the next twenty minutes joy climbing the rocky slopes.

"Let's go!" Nash yelled over the side before starting the trek to our campsite.

I climbed to the top of the mesa and bounced alongside him until I spotted his old rust bucket of a truck. Then, I shifted and dressed while he broke down camp. "You want to get huevos rancheros? I saw a sign for a roadside café when we passed Las Cruces on our way here."

Nash grunted, which I took as a yes. By the time I climbed in the cab, Nash already had the air conditioning on full blast. "It's not even hot out, you know." March in the desert usually meant seventy-degree weather, but this week had been unseasonably warm. But without the humidity I'd grown used to in Kansas City, the eighties felt lovely.

"I'm wearing layers," he grumbled, indicating his standard

grunge wear of worn blue jeans, a wrinkled flannel, and a dark t-shirt. "Where are we headed?"

I stared at him.

"Where are we headed after we stop for food?" he amended.

I flicked the collar of his shirt. "Unless you want to drown, we need to get you a pair of swimming trunks."

Nash cranked the air down and pulled onto the dirt road that would take us to the highway. "Swimming trunks?"

"Or speedos." I shrugged. "Your call."

He snorted. "For what?"

"You'll see." I turned the radio on and flipped through the channels until I landed on Selena's classic "La Carcacha." I'd give Nash the specifics over eggs and chilies. For now, I sang along with Selena, the echo of my dad's deep baritone lurking in the beat.

CHAPTER 2

*D*espite Nash's reservations about dining in a grime-covered old gas station, the roadside diner delivered on its promise of the best huevos rancheros north of the border. I moaned as I stuffed another bite into my mouth.

Nash shook his head but guarded his eggs when I attempted to spear one with my fork. "Let's go over it again." He reached for his second cup of coffee and stared at me.

I waved my fork in the air. "All we have to do is float down the Rio Grande until we spot an adobe house adorned with flowers."

Nash snorted. "This is New Mexico. We've passed a lot of adobe houses. That doesn't narrow it down."

I sipped my freshly squeezed orange juice, relishing the sugar buzz after two days subsisting on expired MREs, dried beef jerky, nuts, and tepid water. Next time Nash and I went camping, I was taking charge of provisions. "We'll know it when we see it," I assured him. After all, we'd already scouted the other two locations that matched New Mexico. Surely, this would be the bedtime story that panned out. I grinned and nudged Nash's foot under the table. "Besides, this one will be fun."

Nash tossed his napkin on his plate, looking unconvinced. "And when we find this flower house, what's the plan to locate the next clue?"

I shrugged. "I'll scout the place and see what turns up. Worst case, I knock on the front door and ask some questions."

"I somehow doubt that'll be the worst case." Nash didn't mention the rattlesnake, but from the look on his face, he was thinking about it.

My phone buzzed on the table with an incoming text from Helen. I held up the screen so Nash could see the picture she'd sent of Garth. Considering the angle of the photo, whoever took it must have been lying on the ground. It looked like a cover for an epic rap album. I was totally going to print it out and add it to my collection of old vinyl record covers displayed on my wall.

Nash squinted at my phone. "Is that a Rottweiler with him?"

"Yup. And a Pomeranian." Garth was in the center of the two dogs, neck feathers ruffled and with a faint brimstone glow in his eyes. He looked badass. Nash watched as I typed a reply to Helen. *Where is he?* I didn't know whose dogs these were.

Magic Paws.

Nash choked on his coffee. "She left a vengeance demon at doggie daycare?"

I grinned and relayed his question.

Instead of a text response, Helen called. "No need to get snippy. It's not a normal doggie daycare." She huffed. "It's very exclusive—supernaturals only."

Even though the diner was almost deserted, I dropped my voice. "Supernatural pets?" I'd never heard of a supernatural dog. I cupped my hand around my mouth to make sure my next question didn't carry. "Are they hellhounds?"

Helen snorted. "The owners are supernaturals, not the dogs, hon."

Well, that made more sense. "And they take roosters?"

"They made an exception in Garth's case," she said.

"They owed you a favor?" I guessed.

She made a noncommittal sound, which meant she had, indeed, called in a favor.

Nash kicked me under the table. Sometimes I forgot he had normal human hearing. That must suck. I caught him up to speed.

Helen hollered at Bea to stop rubbernecking the gym next door. "Leg day," she explained. Helen and the girls had turned watching squats into a spectator sport. "Anyway, Garth wanted to go."

I pushed my empty plate aside. "He told you that, huh?"

"He pecked the little hairs out of my arm every time I drove past, so yes, he told me. Besides, Bea's new cat keeps trying to groom him. He's already chased her around the Stitch Witch once during a quilting demo for a ladies' group. You'd think those Overland Park pearl-clutchers had never seen a chicken before the way they freaked out." She harrumphed. "He needed something to do. I think he misses commanding legions of demons. He's gathered followers already," she said proudly. "He even guards the workers when vamp clients come in to pick up their pets."

I hoped Garth wouldn't encounter any vamps hosting his enemies. I'd have to ask Dez if demons recognized each other while inhabiting human hosts. Garth might look like a heritage breed show rooster, but that little dude could hold a grudge longer than Helen. "How do you know what he does at doggie daycare?" I asked.

"Pet cam. Magic Paws has them set up in the main yard, so we can check up on him throughout the day. You didn't think I'd trust just anyone to take care of him, did you? Kali recommended it. Junior goes there."

As much as Kali babied her Chihuahua, she'd definitely vetted the place. After a full recounting of Garth's daycare escapades, which included spurring a bitey cocker spaniel and destroying four leashes, we said our goodbyes.

"I don't need to know," Nash said before I could tell him all about it. "Let's focus on hunting down these clues so we can retrieve that artifact."

As the vessel mentioned in a demon prophecy, Zagan's chalice could either be used to prevent a demon invasion or to enable it. If the vampires who were searching for it on behalf of the remaining demon kings got to the chalice before we did, they could use it to open the veil between our world and the demon realm. The Enclave may have grudgingly allowed me recovery time over the last few weeks, but Kage Sato's requests for status updates were becoming terser by the week. We needed to secure that artifact soon.

Plus, the sooner we got our hands on the chalice, the quicker we'd get paid. I could use a payday. Since I'd dumped a boatload of money into our headquarters' remodel, my bank account looked pretty sad these days. And Nash blew his paycheck rebuilding vehicles. He'd started with his old beater of a truck before expanding to a 1968 Dodge Charger he'd bought off Autotrader for a steal.

We spent the next ten minutes going over my mom's bedtime story to make sure I hadn't left out any pertinent details. While Nash got up to pay for our check since I'd picked up the last one, my phone buzzed. This time, it lit up with a picture of Dez wearing a superhero cape and flashing his fangs. It'd taken several Bloody Marys to convince him to pose for the photo, and it made me smile every time I saw it.

"Good. I caught you," Dez said when I answered the call.

"Miss me already?" I teased. Although Dez and Nash had graduated to the bickering siblings' stage of their bromance, the mention of camping had been enough for Dez to pass on the invitation to tag along on this trip.

"Yesterday, Bea coerced me into videotaping her afternoon pole dancing class for her social media account." Dez lowered his voice. "It was eighties themed. The decade, not the participants—not that they were much younger."

I laughed. "Did Ruth wear the sparkly thong leotard with the hot pink leg warmers?" Ruth was a sweet seventy-two-year-old witch with an exhibitionist streak. She'd modeled her thrift store find for Bea and the girls before I left for this trip.

"You could've warned me," Dez grumbled.

"Where's the fun in that?"

"Anyway, that's not why I called."

I sat up straighter at his serious tone. "What's up?"

"I've been combing through Bellarose's records to see if I could tie her to those blood runes like you asked."

We all knew she was behind them, but proving it to the Enclave was another matter. Hopefully, Dez had found a smoking gun. Martha Matthews had been the witch peddling blood runes, including the ones that gave Owen Hughes the confidence to challenge Max Volkov to a dominance fight during the shifter tournament. But there was no doubt Zara Bellarose controlled the operation. Few witches were powerful enough to bind blood runes to the air surrounding an object rather than carving them directly into it. That, combined with the illusion magic, which enabled Hughes to flip-shift during his fight with Volkov, required the kind of magical firepower Bellarose was notorious for.

I gestured for Nash to sit down when he returned to the table. "What did you find?" I asked Dez.

"Nothing damning yet, but I put a trace on all of her known credit and debit cards. She used one of those cards two days ago in Roswell."

I swore. Whether she had surveillance on me to see when I left for a job or she had someone close to the Enclave tipping her off, she kept turning up. "Bellarose is coming after the artifact. You think she's following us?"

"She's either got a tracker on Nash's rust bucket, or she's tracing your cell signals."

"Alright. We'll ditch them. I'll text you the new number when I get a burner." I sighed, lamenting the loss of all the playlists I had on this phone.

"I'll keep monitoring her cards."

Nash scanned the street outside the diner as he stood. "I can go out the back, do recon."

I shook my head. "Nah. You'll never spot her." With Bellarose's ability to cast elaborate illusions, he wouldn't see her even if she were standing in front of him. Either I'd have to brush up against everyone in the vicinity to break through the illusion, or we'd have to outsmart her. "Come on. I've got a better idea."

CHAPTER 3

*T*he Riverfront Motel might sound like a vacation resort, but the place smelled like cabbage farts. Even so, it was perfect for the distraction we needed. I handed Nash my fancy new platinum card. Thanks to Dez's handiwork, I now boasted a sterling credit record that allowed me to trade in my five-hundred-dollar secured card. This baby had a credit limit higher than my old bartender salary. "Put the room on the expense account. I'll call for the pizza."

Despite having my name on it, this wasn't the type of motel that matched the name to an ID. Nash handed me his cell phone, took the card, and headed for the front office. By the time he'd returned, I'd found a local pizza joint offering specialty pizzas and called in my order.

Nash grabbed both our bags from the back of his truck and tossed me a key on an oversized keychain.

I dangled it from my finger. "A key? Really?"

"This dump hasn't upgraded anything since the sixties."

I followed him to a room at the end of a rickety walkway

on the second level. "Wow." I eyed the blue velvet bed, complete with a slot to put quarters in to make it vibrate.

"Don't touch the mattress unless you want bed bugs. Or worse." Nash dumped our bags in the bathtub, not willing to risk them touching any carpeted or upholstered surface. He was practical like that. He returned to toss me one of his t-shirts.

"I've got shirts of my own, you know."

He'd already exchanged his flannel shirt for a gray t-shirt. "Yeah, but mine will be baggy enough no one watching for you will look twice."

He had a point. Rather than donning his shirt, I turned around and snapped a quick selfie with the bed in the background and sent it to Max Volkov with a text. *Wish you were here.* While we were chasing clues in New Mexico, Volkov was in New York for business, no doubt staying in the type of hotel that came with a uniformed doorman and left little mints on your silk pillowcase.

It didn't take long to get a reply. *Do you need money?*

I laughed. *Only if it's in quarters.*

There was a lengthy pause, followed by a dire warning about sleeping on the bed or trusting the locks in seedy motels. Not wanting him to worry, I assured him it was merely a pit stop and that I'd call him later tonight. For now, I kept the details vague. While I didn't think Bellarose had the skills to intercept my messages, I wasn't taking any chances.

When the delivery guy arrived, I chatted with him long enough that anyone tailing us would see me tip him and take the cardboard box into the motel room. Then, I put on the baggy t-shirt and dug into the pizza.

Nash already had a rappelling rope dangling out the back

window and down the side of the building. This place might be a dump, but it was old enough to have functional windows, which was the only feature I cared about.

I folded a slice of pizza in half and took a big bite. "So good." I held the box open for Nash.

He waved me off. "No time. Come on." He jerked his head toward the window.

"There's always time for pork and green chili pizza," I mumbled, swiping a second slice before depositing the box on the dresser, which Nash had looped the rope around for an anchor. "You think that'll hold?"

He ducked into the bathroom and returned with a baseball cap for him and a blue bandana for me. "It'll be fine. Let's go."

Even though I was the better climber, Nash insisted on going first. Because that gave me time to eat my second slice of gooey goodness, I didn't argue. I tied the bandana around my hair, tucking the bright pink strands underneath, and climbed through the open window.

As soon as my boots hit the ground, Nash yanked one end of the rope to pull it down and stashed it behind an over-flowing dumpster. "What's the plan?"

"First, we need to score a burner phone and some disguises." I ignored his flinch. The last time he'd allowed Kali and me to put him in a disguise, it had required a shave and a hair-cut. We didn't have time for a full makeover today, though. I pointed. "There's a truck stop about a block that way."

We crossed the lot behind the motel and walked through a strip mall boasting a liquor store with bars on the window, a payday loan place promising predatory interest, and several shuttered businesses. The truck stop offered prepaid cell phones along with a clearance rack filled with ugly swimwear left over from last season. Although Nash vetoed the star-spangled speedo I held up, he grudgingly agreed to the orange board shorts. I grabbed a second pair for myself. Unlike the picked-over swimwear, there was a solid assortment of camouflage apparel to choose from. By the time we headed outside to wait for the rideshare I'd arranged using my new phone, we looked like duck hunters.

Our ride dropped us off at the faded sign for River Rats near the Mesilla Valley Bosque State Park. Two weeks earlier, and we would've been hiking down the sandy Rio Grande riverbed rather than floating. In this part of New Mexico, the water only flowed during irrigation season. Fortunately for us, that began in early March.

River Rats was little more than a shack offering budget float gear. Keeping a low profile mattered more than renting newer equipment, and the bored expression of the guy rummaging through the shack promised he'd forget us as soon as we left. When we declined the grungy lifejackets, he shrugged. According to him, the easy portion of the float lasted about two hours, with some stretches of moderate difficulty if we continued down the river. We passed on his offer to arrange a specific pickup location in favor of calling a ride share, since we had no idea where we'd find the house featured in my mom's bedtime story.

After paying for our tube rental in cash, we changed into our swim shorts in the outdoor bathrooms. Paired with my cheery yellow sports bra, I looked a little less traffic cone and more retro chic. When Nash came out, he held open the plastic grocery bag so I could stuff my clothes inside. He double-bagged the contents to keep everything dry and looped his belt through the handles to attach to his tube. Before he could object, I pulled Nash into a side hug and snapped a photo of us for the group chat.

He glared at me. "Why?"

"Dude, you have actual abs under all that grunge. No one is going to believe it without photographic evidence."

He grunted and tossed me a bottle of water and a bag of peanuts without comment before launching his tube. A few minutes later, we were floating lazily down the river, enjoying the afternoon temps climbing into the seventies. The dry heat was one of the things I missed most about living in New Mexico, and I soaked up as much sunshine as I could while still scanning for adobe houses. Because it was a weekday in March, we were the only ones braving the chilly water.

For the next forty minutes, we floated in companionable silence, the sound of the water and the wildlife soothing away the stress of the past weeks. I'd almost dozed off when my tube snagged on something under the water, ripping a hole in the sun-faded tube and dumping me into the river.

"Shit." I sputtered. The chill chased the last of my drowsiness away. I caught the deflated tube before it was swept off.

"You okay?" Nash called.

"I'm fine," I grumbled, swimming for the bank.

Nash climbed out of the water downriver and waited for me. One glance at my ruined tube, and he grimaced. "Looks like we're walking from here, kiddo."

I sat on the dusty ground. "We might as well eat our snacks first." I ripped open the bag of salted peanuts and tossed a few into my mouth.

Nash joined me without an argument. Thanks to the mid-afternoon sun, our swimming clothes were almost dry by the time we finished eating. Without a house in sight, we took turns dressing behind a scraggly salt cedar. Nash didn't bother with his long-sleeved flannel this time.

Nash held up our new burner phone, angling it in every

direction. "No signal. Cell coverage has been patchy out here." While I'd been practically napping in the water, he must've been checking. He tossed the phone into the plastic grocery bag on top of our damp clothes. After taking a long drink, he added the bottle to the bag and turned to me. "Your mom give you any idea how far we need to go?"

We'd already passed most of the landmarks mentioned in the bedtime story. "From what I can remember, I don't think it should be too far now."

He frowned at the vegetation growing along the river. "I haven't seen many flowers. Do they even grow here this time of year?"

I shrugged. "I guess we'll find out."

We sacrificed the hefty deposit in favor of abandoning the tubes by the tree we'd changed behind and started walking. Two single-wide trailers, half a dozen ranch houses, and one school bus-turned-camper later, I stopped in my tracks.

"An adobe house covered in flowers." A pang of grief hit me as I stared at it. I'd been expecting to find the spiked blooms of red yuccas, shrubs of flowering Russian sage, maybe even the vibrant yellow flowers of a Mexican Bird of Paradise plant—all common sights in this dry, desert climate.

But the small adobe structure wasn't surrounded by living flowers. Instead, a giant mural of delicate white and purple jewel flowers painted the adobe walls. Those small urn-shaped flowers had been my mother's favorite, the same flowers I now wore inked on my calf. As a child, she'd told me one day I'd grow like they did, wild and beautiful in the face of adversity. True strength, she said, didn't come wrapped in muscle and bone but rather from a resilient spirit wise enough to bend when the world would break it.

I wiped away the tears tracking down my cheeks and

sucked in several deep breaths, the dry New Mexico air one more reminder of all I'd lost. And I allowed myself a moment to grieve what I now understood. She must've known her time with me would be cut short. Like the stories she'd regaled me with while I was tucked safely in my bed, even her compliments had been preparing me for what was to come.

CHAPTER 4

*B*ehind the house, a dusty billboard heralded new exhibits at the New Mexico Museum of Art, a museum I'd visited countless times with my parents. I smiled. "Looks like we're going to Santa Fe."

We walked five miles before managing a decent enough cell signal to call for a ride. Because we decided to circle back for Nash's truck after our trip to Santa Fe, we had the driver drop us off at a car rental place on the outskirts of Las Cruces. Even if Bellarose wasn't still watching the truck, we didn't have the equipment to sweep for bugs.

While Nash arranged our transportation, I called Volkov to update him on our progress, as promised. "How's New York City?"

"Crowded." Wherever he was, it must've been outside because there was plenty of traffic noise. "A few more days of this. Then I'll be happy to head home." Most shifters craved wide open spaces over big city living, so it wasn't surprising Volkov preferred his house in a rural subdivision backed by acres of trees over a view of skyscrapers. The traffic noise quieted as he moved inside. "There's something big brewing, though."

I shifted the phone to my shoulder so I could dig my credit card out for Nash to pay for our car rental. "What do you mean?"

"After my meeting with the New York pack yesterday, I attended an invitation-only auction to bid on a set of rare books for my collection." Although he hadn't mentioned the auction before, it didn't surprise me it was part of his itinerary. Volkov's library was a thing of beauty, with floor-to-ceiling dark wood bookcases and an oversized stone fireplace. He filled it with everything from shifter history to rare magical tomes. "Typically," he explained, "all the major power players bid for books like these."

"But they didn't?"

"Everyone except the vampires."

I frowned. "They weren't interested?"

"There wasn't a vampire in attendance," he said. "Rumor on the street is that the vamp council is at odds, and they're only interested in bidding for demon artifacts these days."

We all knew the vamps would love to get their hands on the artifacts I was chasing. That was nothing new. But they hadn't been singularly focused on acquiring them until now. "You think they know something we don't?"

"I think they know more about this prophecy than we do." A hint of a growl came through, and I could practically see him raking a hand through his dark hair in frustration. Volkov was a man used to controlling insider information, not being locked out of it. And when it came to anything that could be a threat to me, he took it personally. "Watch your back, Riley."

"Always," I promised. When I told him about our tail, Volkov swore. "And you're sure you lost her?"

"Yeah. Dez called while we were waiting for our ride. He checked the traffic cam footage near the locations Bellarose used her credit card to identify her car. Then, he hacked into her onboard navigation to track her. He said her vehicle hasn't moved from the Riverfront Motel. Dez will let me know the second she's on the move again."

"Good. Don't go to the motel." He used the bossy alpha voice that made me want to do the opposite, but since he was worried, I let it slide. "You keep the rental car. I'll send someone to drive Nash's truck to KC." Volkov said it as if sending someone to retrieve the truck was a quick errand.

"You don't need to do that, Max. We can come back for it."

"It's no trouble," he insisted.

I laughed. "It's a nine-hundred-mile trip from Kansas City to Las Cruces."

The man wasn't easily deterred. "Listen, I've got a shifter visiting Nate Irons' pack in El Paso to lend tech support. I'll have one of Irons' wolves drop Arlo in Las Cruces and drive the truck home tonight."

I bit my lip. It would be nice not to have to backtrack. Because Dez turned feral at the mention of his competition's name, I'd be sure to keep Arlo's involvement to myself. I covered the phone and relayed Volkov's offer to Nash. "You good with someone else driving your baby?" It might be a rust bucket, but Nash loved that truck like I loved green chilies.

While he didn't look happy about it, the idea of spending any more time in New Mexico than necessary must've been worse because he agreed.

"Alright," I told Volkov. "But the keys aren't in the truck." I wracked my brain for a secure place to leave them for Arlo that wouldn't require us going back to the motel.

Volkov chuckled. "Trust me. That won't be a problem for Arlo. It'll be waiting at my place when you get back."

Despite feeling a twinge of disloyalty to Dez, learning Arlo could hot-wire cars in addition to being a techy nerd made it hard not to like the guy. "Thanks. I'll see you soon."

"Not soon enough." He paused. "Be careful, Riley."

"You too."

Nash dropped a heavy hand on my shoulder and steered me toward the door as I hung up. "The sooner we get this done, the sooner you two can go back to making the rest of us uncomfortable with your PDA."

I didn't deny it. Ever since Volkov confessed he'd known we were mates from the day he met me, he'd been more hands-on than usual. I loved those hands on me, so I wasn't complaining. Nash and Dez, however, gave me shit about it like middle schoolers. "Pfft. I need to set you up on a date, so you won't be such a grump about PDA."

"Hard pass." Nash headed toward a nondescript dark gray sedan parked in the rental car lot. "I can only imagine the woman you'd set me up with."

I clutched my hand to my heart as if I were mortally wounded. He kept walking. Nash unlocked the car and tossed his rumpled grocery bag in the back.

"You want me to drive?" I teased.

Nash shot me an over-my-dead-body look as he got in the driver's seat. "I've had enough brushes with death for one trip."

"Oh please," I scoffed. "One little rattlesnake trapped in a backpack hardly qualifies as a brush with death." I climbed into the passenger side and fiddled with the radio, settling on a classic country station I knew Nash would like.

Within minutes, Las Cruces was in the rearview mirror. Between bathroom breaks and a dinner pit stop, the drive to Santa Fe took a little over five hours. By the time we arrived, my legs were stiff, and our destination was closed for the day. We checked into lodging that was a definite upgrade from the Riverfront Motel. I hit up the vending machines for late-night snacks before crashing.

The next morning, we were waiting outside the doors when the New Mexico Museum of Art opened. Located on the plaza, the museum was a sprawling pueblo-style building reminiscent of the old adobe mission churches found throughout the Southwest. It boasted an impressive art collection, with several galleries surrounding a courtyard. We started on the first floor.

Nash stopped in front of a contemporary photography exhibit, examining each piece carefully before scratching his bearded cheek. "Any idea what we're looking for?"

"Not really," I admitted. "I'm hoping I'll know when I see it —like the last clue."

Nothing in the photos sparked a memory, so we moved into the next room. An hour later, we'd examined most of the galleries and the St. Francis Auditorium with no luck.

Nash waited until the couple studying a storyteller exhibit moved across the room before turning to me. "Recognize anything?"

"Not yet." I blew out a frustrated breath, watching the couple open the door to the courtyard. "It looks like there's more art out there. We should check it out."

We followed the couple outside. The open courtyard included covered walkways on all four sides, with fresco murals adorning the walls. Well-tended garden plants filled the courtyard. It was a lovely space, but there was nothing that sparked a memory here.

I gestured toward a closed door. "Let's hope it's in there." If we didn't find the clue in this last gallery, we'd have to go through the entire museum again and again until we located it.

My stomach rumbled. Maybe after lunch. We'd been anxious to get here before Bellarose caught up to us, which meant we'd settled for a sad vending machine breakfast. Luckily, there were several restaurants nearby. My parents had worked at a couple of them, but they'd all been too expensive for us to eat at when I was a child.

There was no place in this city that didn't dredge up memories. Some of them, like the linen-covered outdoor tables on the plaza, made me feel closer to my parents. Others, like the gated neighborhoods we'd passed on our way here, brought back darker memories of the jobs my old alpha sent me on. Even though I'd killed Carl with my own hand, so much of my life here had been tainted by him, including the heartache of losing my parents.

I followed Nash across the courtyard to the final gallery. We both spotted the oil painting as soon as we walked inside.

"Isn't that the same painting that was on the billboard?" Nash asked.

A buzz of excitement drew me to it. "Yeah. It is."

The painting depicted a vibrant New Mexico sunset over the Santa Fe skyline. Nostalgia rose as I gazed at it. Often on summer nights, my dad would cup his hands to give me a boost, so I could scramble up the trellis attached to our rental house. He'd climb up after me, and we'd sit on the roof, watching the sun paint the sky. Even a run-down neighborhood was beautiful in the right light.

"You okay?" Nash patted me awkwardly on the arm as I stood there teary-eyed. "Do you need a hug or something?" He sounded horrified by the prospect, but he offered anyway.

I wiped my eyes on the hem of my shirt and laughed. "I'm alright. Reminds me of my parents, that's all."

Nash's relaxed, off the hook for hug duty. "This must be the clue, then. Any idea what it means?"

Turning to the painting, I studied it before reading the plaque below it. My breath caught at the artist's name. "Maria Baca." I stared at Nash. "Maria was the woman who rented studio space to my mother here in Santa Fe."

A few months ago, I'd returned to her studio, and Maria had given me the ring I now wore. My mom left it with instructions to give it to me if something happened to her. Although Maria had searched for me after my parents' deaths, Carl had made sure I stayed off the radar. It hadn't been until I came back for the Alatyr stone Nash wore now around his neck as a talisman that she'd given the ring to me.

This ring was nothing like the elegant jewelry my mother normally crafted. I twisted the silver ring around my finger, tracing the inlaid copper and the runes she'd etched into its surface. Were these runes the next clue? Or was there something else hidden at my mother's old studio? Something even Maria hadn't known to give me.

There was only one way to find out.

CHAPTER 5

I prepared myself for everything save the devastation we found. The last time I'd visited this studio, Maria Baca's warmth infused the space, from the vibrant paintings to the scent of the sandalwood incense she loved to burn. When I'd walked through these doors months ago, Maria had greeted me like I'd never left, the faint laugh lines bracketing her lips and the silver in her dark braid the only signs she'd aged since I'd last seen her. She'd been my only remaining connection to my mother.

When I'd come here with Volkov, we hadn't had time for more than a quick visit though. The need to get the Alatyr stone to Kansas City to save Nash's life had trumped my desire to spend time catching up. I'd promised her I'd come back. I thought I had time.

From the state of this place, I wasn't so sure I'd get the chance. There was no sign of Maria here. And there was no hint of warmth in the scene that greeted us now. While Nash served as lookout, I made quick work of the lock. Inside, the studio had been destroyed—her paintings slashed and pottery shattered on the tile floor. So much beauty lay in ruins at our feet.

Anger simmered as I surveyed the studio. Whoever did this had inflicted maximum damage. No piece of art was untouched. I picked up an easel and sat it upright before placing a torn canvas on it. I inspected the windows. "No sign of forced entry." They either picked the lock like I did, securing the door as they left, or someone let them in. My pulse sped up as I searched for any indication of a struggle. There was no blood, which was good, but given the debris strewn around the room, it was hard to tell if there'd been a fight.

Nash nudged a broken sculpture with the toe of his cowboy boot. "Someone tosses a place like this, it usually means they were looking for something," he said.

I glanced at my mother's ring on my finger. "You think it's related to my mom's will? To the artifact we're hunting?"

"Possibly." Nash walked the perimeter of the room, stopping in front of a metal fire safe recessed into the wall. The painting that must've hidden it was lying on the floor below it. He tapped the metal. "Strange they didn't take this."

I ducked under his arm and put my ear to the safe. Not that I needed to. The combination was Maria's birthday, same as it had been when I was a child and she'd locked my marble collection in it for safekeeping. "Empty."

"How hard is it to crack a cheap safe like this?" he asked.

"Cake walk for anyone who's watched a few online videos and has the time to mess around with it." I closed the safe. "But why close and lock it?" I gestured to the rest of the room. "It's not like they tried to hide that they were here."

Nash scanned the mess. "You think Maria emptied the safe? Ran before they got here?"

"Maybe. But that still doesn't explain why they didn't either break into it or bust it out of the wall to take with them."

"Unless they were interrupted," Nash reasoned.

"Or they weren't here to steal something." I picked up another canvas, this one sliced to ribbons. "Whoever did this wanted to make a point. Tossing a place doesn't require destroying the artwork."

"Since Bellarose has been tailing us, it probably wasn't her." Nash gestured to the trashed room. "Could be that this has nothing to do with you or your mother's will."

"That's possible," I conceded, not believing it for a second. The timing of this was too suspect, mere weeks after the Enclave got their hands on the will and the letter my mother left for me here in Santa Fe. "But it's also possible someone at the lawyer's office handling my mother's will talked about it to the wrong person."

Nash shot me a considering look. "I take it a lot of supernaturals would recognize how valuable that information is."

A vampire could easily compel the lawyer to repeat the will verbatim. I mentally ran through the wording of the letter she'd left me. My mother had been smart to avoid mentioning the artifact or demons directly. However, it'd been clear that whatever she had left was something of immense value only I could locate.

"Exactly." Knowing who I was and what I did for Carl would be enough to make local supernaturals assume it was a rare artifact. "And if the wrong person recognized the value of what was in her will, they could sell the information to one of the power players."

"And we're back to Bellarose," Nash said.

"Or Damien Creed." Since Creed lived in Santa Fe, it

wasn't a stretch to think that he'd found out about the will. He had eyes and ears all over the city. And he certainly knew the kind of work I did for Carl since one of the artifacts I'd stolen had been in Creed's possession. I glanced at the shark tooth necklace Nash wore to disguise the chip of the Alatyr stone.

Nash circled the room, examining the destruction. "Okay, so either Zara Bellarose or Damien Creed could have done this."

"Yes." Even as I said it, Volkov's warning rang in my ears. "Or it could be a vampire going after it for their king. It's not exactly a secret that I retrieve demon artifacts for the Enclave. Anyone who knows that could guess what kind of object I'd be after. We know the remaining demon kings are searching for these artifacts and that the vessel my mom hid is supposedly the linchpin to this prophecy. All the kings will have vamps loyal to them hunting it."

When the demon kings banded together to kill Beleth in the last demon war, it created a power vacuum. Beleth had served as high king in addition to leading the temptation demons. Each of the remaining five kings led a legion populated by a type of demon—divination, vengeance, war, deception, and chaos. After killing Beleth, they sent vampires loyal to them to hide several objects of power in the human world. Almost immediately, they each began their search to acquire them and take the empty throne.

According to the prophecy, whichever demon controlled the items needed to tear down the veil between their world and ours would reign supreme over both worlds. Although the Enclave refused to share the full prophecy, we knew some components from the jobs they'd sent me on—weapons forged in hellfire that could kill any demon, a dangerous spell book, an elemental child who could wield both water and air, and the vessel my mother had hidden.

Fortunately, my mom was clever enough to leave a trail only I could follow. "Whoever did this wouldn't recognize the clue even if they found it." I pointed to the opposite side of the room where a door led into Maria's office. "You go through Maria's desk, see if you can find a home address for her. I'll search the studio to see if I can turn up the next clue."

Nash nodded and got to work. It took us about an hour to search. While there was nothing that appeared to be a clue, Nash found a stack of mail with a residential address on the south side of Santa Fe. Despite the dread spreading through my body, I forced myself to get in the rental car, so we could check it out. Everything I knew about Maria told me she'd never leave her studio in this state. The fact it was in shambles meant there was a good chance we wouldn't find her alive.

I spent the drive to the middle-class neighborhood lost in memories of my mom and Maria, their heads bent close together as they shared secrets and laughter. I recalled them working side by side in this studio, both women so absorbed in their art that they'd lose all track of time. My dad and I would come looking for my mom when she didn't make it home for dinner. Back then, I hadn't realized his relief at finding her in the studio might be about more than a husband's normal worries.

I wondered again if he'd known who Amelia had been and what she'd done before us. As we drove to Maria Baca's home, I hoped my mother's secrets hadn't gotten her best friend killed all these years later.

CHAPTER 6

The sold sign in the front yard gave me hope Maria made it out of Santa Fe in one piece. Her neighbors told us she put her house on the market suddenly, the moving truck coming not long after. Everyone had their own theory of where she moved. The elderly man who lived next door believed she moved to be closer to family while the middle-aged couple across the street swore she came into money and upgraded to a fancy gated community somewhere in California. Wherever she went, she'd left in a hurry. None of them had seen her since.

"We didn't find the clue at her studio, and her place is empty." Nash turned on the air conditioning to combat the afternoon sun heating up our rental car as we sat in Maria's empty driveway. "Now what?"

I dropped my head against the back of the seat and turned toward him. "Now, we go home."

He eyed the ring glinting in the sunlight. "You think that ring is the clue."

"I do." I tamped down the frustration at the thought that we'd traipsed through New Mexico for a week when the clue had been on my finger this whole time. But it made sense. Maria said she'd held this ring for me all these years because it was important to my mother I have it. I studied the runes. "These must be the clue, but I have no idea what they mean."

"Time to enlist the help of your witches," Nash said.

"Yes." Helen and the girls had already conducted a preliminary search with no luck. Between the shifter summit and battling Martha Matthews' quest to force me into her coven, we'd all become too preoccupied to focus on deciphering them. Now that I suspected my job hinged on these runes, as well as the fate of the world, I'd ask Helen to call in some favors to gain access to the Kansas City coven's extensive library. And I'd hit up Volkov's personal library to see whether any of the rare books in his collection cataloged lesser-known runes.

I called Dez on the drive home and asked him to search for any trace of Maria Baca. There might be nothing left for me in Santa Fe, but I needed to know she made it out of there okay. At midnight, we stopped in Dodge City long enough to get a solid six hours of sleep before driving the rest of the way home.

By the time we hit Kansas City, it was early afternoon. Because I'd already fielded one call from Kage Sato on the drive demanding a progress update, I decided to bypass my place and head straight to Volkov's house instead to do some research. Nash had to get his truck, anyway.

"You can leave the car with me," I suggested as he turned off I-70. "I'll drop it off."

Nash laughed. "I don't think so. I want my deposit back, and I've heard all about your driving, kiddo." He pulled onto a familiar street, parking in front of Dez's upscale apartment complex. We waited for the tattletale to climb in the backseat, his laptop tucked under one arm.

As soon as Dez closed the door, I turned around to face him. "My driving isn't that bad."

Dez's eyes widened behind his black-framed glasses, and his mouth dropped open. "You're a terrible driver," he finally managed. "The one time I was a passenger, I thought we'd both die."

"You're such a drama llama. It was my first time driving. Besides," I looked pointedly at Nash, "your eye was swollen shut because Nash clocked you, so how much could you even see?"

Dez's cheeks flushed as he buckled his seat belt. "One eye was enough to watch you swerve off the road and smash into Hopper's truck." Dez glared at the back of Nash's head at the reminder of his black eye. Since we'd been robbing Nash, the punch had been justified. Fortunately, with all the gym time Dez had been putting in, he was better at dodging punches these days.

Nash sighed and pulled into traffic. "We'll pick up my truck first." He used his no-nonsense Green Beret voice to change the subject. "Dez will drop off the rental, and I'll follow to give him a ride home. You want me to drop you at headquarters?"

"Nah. I'm staying at Volkov's house tonight." Volkov wouldn't get home until later, but I had his library and his swanky shower, complete with a rainfall showerhead and aromatherapy, to keep me company.

Plus, I'd missed waking up next to him. While I'd been recovering from my stab wound, he'd stayed at my place every night. I hadn't slept well since we left for New Mexico. Part of that I blamed on Nash's snoring like a freight train. But mostly I missed Max's strong arms wrapped around me and his solid chest at my back.

Dez handed me a slip of paper with a number scrawled on it.

"What's this?" I asked.

"That's the home phone number for Maria Baca's daughter, who lives in Bakersfield, California. Maria left a forwarding address at the post office."

A wave of relief swept through me. Whatever happened in that studio, Maria hadn't been harmed. I flipped down the visor, so I could see Dez in the mirror. "Thank you."

"No problem." He opened his laptop. "I've also been monitoring Zara Bellarose's location through her car's GPS. Yesterday, she must've abandoned the motel stakeout, probably when someone picked up Nash's truck." He frowned and caught my gaze in the mirror. "Who did pick up Nash's truck?"

When I'd told him we left the truck for a rental, I'd left out the details. "One of Volkov's pack members was in El Paso," I hedged.

Dez returned to typing on his laptop. "Bellarose's car drove straight to a private airfield in Albuquerque. I assume she flew back to Toronto. How do you think she found out you were in New Mexico, anyway?"

I shrugged. "We didn't advertise why we were going, but we weren't secretive about the trip either. Our current theory is that someone in Santa Fe heard about my mom's will and sold the info. If Bellarose knew I was going after the artifact, it would've been pretty simple to bug Nash's truck."

Dez smirked. "One benefit of driving an old junker is there's no way to hack into the non-existent GPS."

Nash smiled. "Exactly." He glanced at me. "I think we've got a leak."

Dez nodded. "Someone associated with the Enclave. Makes sense."

The thought had occurred to me, especially since they tried to force me into Martha Matthews' coven. I spun the ring on my finger. "When we figure out what these runes mean, I say we keep that info and our next steps to ourselves until we secure the artifact. In the meantime, I'll keep my status reports to Sato vague."

"Or," Nash grinned, "you feed him bullshit and see if he's our leak."

"Good idea." Because the man meant something to Max's brother Aleksei, I hoped it wasn't him. But Kage Sato was hard to get a read on. Years as a spy and assassin perfected his poker face. "Any chance you could keep tabs on Bellarose?" I asked Dez. "We need to know what she's up to."

"Working on it."

Unable to wait any longer, I dialed the phone number Dez gave me. An unfamiliar voice answered on the second ring. "Hi. I'm trying to get in touch with Maria Baca."

"And who is this?" the woman asked.

"Riley Cruz. Maria was a close friend of my mother."

After a beat of silence, Maria's voice came online. "Riley? What's wrong?"

I told her about my mother's will, my hunt for clues, and the state we found her studio in. Turns out, Maria didn't know her place had been trashed. After handing off the ring my mother had entrusted to her safekeeping, she'd put her house on the market. When her daughter called to ask if she'd come stay with her while she recovered from surgery, Maria moved her furniture and belongings to a storage unit and headed to California. She'd planned on coming back to close up the studio next month. After talking to her for a few minutes, it was clear she had no idea what my mother might have left for me other than the ring I already wore.

Thanks to that call, I felt lighter than I had in days when Nash dropped me off at Volkov's house. I might not know what this last clue meant yet, but I'd figure it out. More importantly, Maria was safe and happy living with her daughter.

I punched the code into Volkov's security system, dreaming of his luxury bathroom and its aromatherapy. But first, I needed fuel, and the state of Volkov's refrigerator made me sad. Since delivery out here was non-existent, I decided to call a rideshare to drive me to the closest grocery store. Might as well stock up. Once Volkov got home, we'd need sustenance for the homecoming I had planned.

As I was typing the address into the rideshare app, the doorbell rang. With any luck, it would be Teagan or another pack member who I could sucker into taking me instead.

I tucked my phone into my pocket and opened the door with a grin. The smile died as soon as I saw who was standing on the other side.

"Irina?"

I wasn't the only one shocked. Irina stared at me, her lips parted and a flicker of panic in her frosty blue eyes.

Volkov would've mentioned his mother's arrival if he'd known she was coming, so this must be a surprise visit. "Is everything okay?" I asked.

Irina regained her composure. "Of course." She glanced at the beautiful woman by her side. Then, she looked at me. "I didn't expect to find you here."

I raised a brow. No. I suppose she didn't. There wasn't a

good response to that, so I let it slide. Not wanting to be rude and ignore the woman with her, I forced a sunny smile. "And who is your friend?"

Irina grimaced, but then she squared her delicate shoulders and met my eyes. "This is Maxim's fiancé."

CHAPTER 7

*U*nable to help myself, I gawked at the stunning woman next to Irina. With shiny chestnut hair styled in perfect loose waves, cheekbones that belonged on a runway, and cornflower blue eyes, she was beauty-pageant pretty. She appeared to be about my age, but that's where the similarities between us ended.

Everything about this woman screamed old money. She was draped in diamonds from ear to wrist. From her cream V-neck to her tailored pants cinched to show off a trim waist, her clothes were flawless. I resisted the urge to glance at the splotch of red from where I'd dropped a meatball on my left boob at lunch.

This was not the homecoming I'd planned.

Still, I held the door open and invited the two women inside. I didn't miss the censure in Irina's eyes when she caught sight of my scuffed combat boots and thrifted *Rage Against the Machine* vintage band tee. The last time I'd seen Max's mother, I'd dressed like a prep school wannabe in an attempt to impress her. Considering how that luncheon went, the combat boots were warranted.

I popped a stick of cinnamon gum in my mouth before extending the pack to them. Neither woman took me up on the offer.

Standing in the foyer, the mystery woman scanned Volkov's house like she was taking inventory while Irina's gaze remained on me. "Is Maxim here?" Irina asked.

"He's out of town on business. But he'll be home tonight if you want to wait." I gestured to the formal seating in the living room rather than inviting them into the library where I'd planned to spend the evening sifting through old books until Volkov arrived. With the present company, I reconsidered that plan.

Neither woman moved toward the living room.

Irina's smile grew strained. "We'll be fine here until my son returns. No need to entertain us. I'm certain you have important things to do." Her tone was exceedingly polite, even as her nostrils flared at the idea of me having important things to occupy me.

I ignored the dismissal and held out my hand to the woman with her. "Hi. I'm Riley."

She hesitated before placing a cool palm against mine. "Nadia." A slight frown marred her perfect brows as she stopped cataloging the house long enough to take in my outfit. "Are you the housekeeper?" She spoke with the same slight Russian accent Irina had.

"She's an associate of Maxim's," Irina rushed in before I had a chance to answer.

I rubbed my temples, wondering if spending time in his mother's presence would always end with a headache. "This isn't a conversation for an empty stomach," I muttered.

Both women stared at me.

I gave up on herding them into the living room. "Do you like barbecue?"

"Pardon?" Nadia asked.

"You know, smoked meats smothered in barbecue sauce."

"I've never tried it," Nadia said.

It was my turn to stare. "Well, that's a damn tragedy." I grabbed the small clutch she'd left on the entry table and thrust it back into Nadia's hands. Then, I opened the front door. "Let's go."

Irina stiffened, her cool blue eyes narrowing. "We're not hungry."

Nadia shifted her gaze between the two of us. "I could eat."

"Great," I said brightly as I peered at the sleek car idling in the driveway. "Did you rent a car?" I'd never seen a luxury car like that at the airport rental place.

Irina followed my gaze. "Of course not. I hired a driver for the duration of our stay." As we watched, a man dressed in a three-piece suit stepped out of the vehicle and stood next to the passenger side door. He looked like the driver from virtually every mob movie I'd ever watched—big, stoic, and good at appearing menacing even while avoiding eye contact.

"Sweet!" I grabbed Nadia's arm and pulled her along with me before she changed her mind. "If Max beats us here, tell him we'll be back soon," I called over my shoulder.

We left Irina standing in the open doorway looking bewildered as Nadia slid into the waiting car. I gave the driver directions to West Bottoms. Once we were both seated, I rolled down the window and waved.

Irina didn't wave back.

Nadia studied me. "You're not a business associate, are you?"

"Nope." I smiled. "And you're not Max's fiancé." I didn't phrase it as a question.

"That depends on who you ask," she said.

"Meaning?"

"Our parents arranged for us to mate when we were children." If it weren't for the brief flare of annoyance that crossed her beautiful face, I would've assumed she was on board. "But I haven't seen Maxim since we were young. Even then, we barely knew each other."

No wonder she didn't look thrilled. Of course, once she saw Max in all his grown-up glory, she might feel differently. "And Irina arranged this little visit hoping to change that," I guessed.

Nadia inclined her head. "After years of barely mentioning it, she suddenly seemed in a hurry for us to mate." Her lips twitched. "Now I understand why."

I sighed. "She's determined. I'll give her that."

Nadia pushed her long dark hair over her shoulder and tilted her head, watching me. "You're not even a little worried he'll choose me, are you?"

"Nah." I winked at her. "That man waited a decade for a first date and face-planted into poison ivy for me. It'd take a helluva lot more than a pretty face and a meddling mother to tear Max from my side."

Her brow furrowed again. "Why did you invite me to dinner then?"

"Mostly to make Irina sweat," I admitted.

Nadia laughed, a little of her ice princess mask slipping. Even her laugh was pretty.

"Plus, it would be a shame if you visited Kansas City without sampling our barbecue." I eyed her cream-colored top. "But we're going to have to make a stop first. You can't eat barbecue dressed like that." I pointed to the red stain on my t-shirt as evidence.

She leaned forward in her seat with a genuine smile. "I love shopping."

I smiled back at her. "You ever been to a thrift store, Nadia?"

She shook her head, but her eyes lit up. "Irina would never step inside one, would she?"

I tried to imagine Max's perfectly polished mother climbing the rickety stairs in a West Bottoms' thrift store to rummage through racks of secondhand clothing and vintage toys. Even my imagination wasn't that good. "Never," I agreed.

Because I didn't want Volkov to be blindsided, I texted to let him know to expect his guests. Seconds after hitting send, my phone rang.

"I'll deal with my mother," Volkov promised.

With her shifter hearing, I may as well have had the phone on speaker. Nadia flinched at the barely leashed fury in Volkov's voice.

Not your fault, I mouthed to her. I was sure Irina didn't warn her about a hostile reception.

"That arranged mating was never going to happen." He put heavy emphasis on the never, his deep voice edged with panic.

"I know," I said softly.

He let out a harsh breath. "You said my mother is at the house. But I can hear traffic. Where are you?"

"Nadia and I are about to go thrifting in West Bottoms before hitting up the food trucks."

Nadia quickly covered her apprehension at the idea of eating parking-lot fare. I wasn't worried. As soon as she tasted the pulled pork, she'd be a fan for life.

I grinned. "We borrowed your mother's driver."

"Of course, you did." The tension I'd been carrying eased at the sound of Volkov's husky laugh. "I love you," he said.

"I know that, too." I glanced out the window as the car rolled to a stop. "I gotta go." I paused. "Don't kill your mom, okay?"

"No promises," he grumbled.

The driver parked in front of Howl. This time of year, Volkov's haunted house only opened for special events, but it was near the bustling first weekend crowd drifting from store to store. Taking up several city blocks, West Bottoms came alive on the weekends. Originally a manufacturing district, the old five-story brick warehouses now held a collection of artists' studios, thrift and specialty shops, and the haunted houses that put this neighborhood on the map. It was also home to my team's recently remodeled headquarters.

The driver opened the door and offered his hand to steady us like we were about to walk the red carpet. I fished in my pocket for a twenty and held it out to him. He blinked down at it and then at me, realization dawning. "No need to tip me, ma'am."

I grimaced. It had taken me months to break Volkov's pack of calling me ma'am. "Riley," I insisted.

From the look on his face, we weren't going to be on a first name basis anytime soon.

Nadia leaned close and whispered. "Irina pays him a generous salary."

I flushed and looked at the crumpled twenty in my hand. "Of course." I stuffed it back in my pocket.

The driver reached into his jacket, pulled out a crisp black business card, and handed it to me. "I'll park around the corner. Call when you're finished shopping, and I'll pick you up."

I led a wide-eyed Nadia into the closest thrift store. The inside of the shop was shabby chic with a sparkling chandelier hanging above an old milk crate filled with metal gas station signs. Four floors held reclaimed furniture, retro clothing, scented candles, and household goods. The top floor was reserved for a pop-up cocktail bar and a collection of old windows, vintage tools, and old post office boxes for sale.

Nadia wandered through the first floor, pausing on the painted wooden stairs leading to the second level. "This place is amazing."

Despite the circumstances, I found myself liking Nadia. Away from Irina, she proved to be far more fun than I would've guessed. She didn't complain once as I passed her increasingly obnoxious outfits under the dressing room door. Although I lobbied hard for the maroon eighties parachute pants and puffy white jacket with an iron-on eagle patch, Nadia walked out dressed like she was my sister. I whistled as she spun in a circle. She wore a snarky t-shirt, dark-washed denim jeans that hugged her long legs, and studded leather boots. And she still looked like a beauty queen.

After Nadia paid for her new bargain-priced wardrobe, I snapped off the tags for her. Then, I hooked my arm with hers, and we followed the divine scent of smoked brisket and pulled pork wafting across the parking lot.

CHAPTER 8

*T*he sound of ice hitting glass was my only warning I was walking into a minefield. One look at Volkov's rigid jaw and white-knuckled hold on the decanter of pricey whiskey told me my timing was shit. I'd hoped to come back after the blowup, not before it.

Both Volkovs looked up as I froze like a gazelle in the open doorway.

Irina spoke first. "Where is Nadia?" She glanced behind me.

I cleared my throat. "Nadia decided to go to a hotel for the night. She said this was a family matter."

"Smart woman." Volkov's arctic blue eyes clashed with his mother's gaze.

She looked away first, clasping her hands together in her lap.

Volkov downed his drink and placed the empty glass on the sideboard before holding a hand out to me. Briefly, I considered bolting, but Helen hadn't raised me to be a coward. Might as well get this over with. I crossed the library, passing Irina who sat ramrod straight like she was carved from stone. Volkov's hand was warm and steady as he pulled me to his side. He pressed a kiss against my temple before facing Irina again.

"Let me make this crystal clear, mother."

From the way Irina flinched, she hadn't been on the receiving end of Volkov's pissed-off alpha voice before. Her gaze skimmed over her son's arm now wrapped around me, and she swallowed.

Volkov pressed me closer to his body. "I'm not playing these games with you. Riley is my mate. You can either accept that, or we are done."

"Max," I whispered. "That's not what I want. It's okay." I didn't need Irina's approval. I had him. That would always be enough.

"It's not okay," he said.

All the color drained from Irina's face as she stared at me. "When?"

I knew what she was asking—when had the mate bond formed between us. A simple question, but a complicated answer thanks to my immunity to magic.

Volkov's wolf rose, those molten amber eyes locking with mine. "The moment I saw her nine years ago."

Just as it had the first time he said it, something warm and bright unfurled inside me.

"I didn't know," Irina whispered.

"You didn't want to know," Volkov challenged.

Irina stiffened before nodding. "I apologize for overstepping." A muscle worked in her jaw as if she had to force the next words out. "I will not disrespect your mate again. If you wish me to leave, I understand. I can go to a hotel as well."

Volkov remained silent, rage still written in the hard lines of his body.

I took a steadying breath and held out the olive branch. I'd lost my mother. No way would I be the cause of Volkov losing his. "Please, stay."

Surprise flashed through Irina's cool blue eyes, but she recovered quickly. "Thank you." She stood on shaky legs. "I will retire for the evening and leave you to your homecoming." Irina held her head high as she glided from the room.

The second we were alone, I wrapped Volkov's tie around my hand and pulled him to me. Our lips crashed together, all the pent-up anger kindling into something fierce and wild. He swept his tongue into my mouth, pulling my body flush against his. I threaded my fingers through his dark hair and kissed him back until we were both breathless.

He shifted his lips to my ear. "Wishing you wouldn't have shut down that offer for her to go to a hotel?"

"Maybe." I dropped my head against his chest and held him a few more minutes. "I missed this."

"Me, too."

When I let go, Volkov shrugged off his jacket and tie. He sat on the leather couch, making room for me. Despite the desire simmering between us, there was no way we were getting naked with his mother in the guest room, so we settled in for an evening of research. After telling Volkov about Maria and about our current theories, we hit the books.

Two hours later, we'd made it through half of the magical section of his collection and were no closer to identifying the runes than when we started. Because Volkov had an early meeting, and we were both exhausted, we left piles of books on the floor for morning. I fell asleep with Volkov's steady heartbeat under my cheek and a nagging feeling I was over-looking something important.

By the time I woke, Volkov's side of the bed was meticu-lously made as if he'd never slept there. My side, on the other hand, sported twisted sheets and a damp spot on the pillow-case where I'd drooled in my sleep. Nice.

I rolled over and stared at the wooden beams on the bedroom ceiling, gathering the will to face Irina Volkov again. I checked the clock. It'd be at least a couple more hours before Volkov made it home. Groaning, I forced myself to get up. After a half-assed attempt at making my side of the bed, I grabbed a change of clothes and killed another half hour in the shower.

When I emerged from the bedroom dressed in ripped blue jeans and a faded t-shirt, Irina already sat at the breakfast nook. She sipped orange juice from a crystal glass, a plate of artfully arranged crepes topped with berries in front of her. She'd barely touched the food, staring out the window at the grove of trees behind Volkov's house.

Irina looked up as I entered the room, her blue eyes wary. Even at seven in the morning, her golden blonde hair was perfectly styled and her outfit elegant.

"Good morning," I said with as much enthusiasm as I could muster.

"Maxim arranged breakfast to be delivered for us." Irina nodded toward a covered dish across the table. When I hesi-tated, she sighed. "Please join me."

Most mornings, I was a cereal girlie. Give me a family-sized box of Lucky Charms, and I was ready to tackle the day. Based on this spread, Irina was accustomed to fancier fare.

As I approached the table, I wondered if this is how Nash

felt when handling that rattlesnake. I served myself, forgoing the crystal for a utilitarian glass filled with ice water from the refrigerator door. For a few minutes, the only sound was the clink of our forks against the bone china plates I'd never seen before. The crepes were the best I'd ever tasted, but they still sat like lead in my belly as the awkward silence stretched between us.

Irina laid her fork on her plate and attempted a smile. "For Maxim's sake, we should make peace."

I couldn't stop the snort. Only one of us viewed our interactions as a battleground, and it sure as shit wasn't me.

Irina's lips thinned, but she persisted. "I was wrong to invite Nadia here." Her expression turned earnest. "Surely, you understand I only want what's best for my son." The "and that's not you" part went unsaid.

I shoved a giant bite of crepe into my mouth to occupy my tongue. At the sound of the doorbell, I leapt to my feet, grateful for any distraction from this conversation.

I opened the door to find Helen and Alyce jostling for position on the porch, trying to peer through the small side window. Both women straightened and gave me their best innocent smiles.

This would be a distraction all right.

Alyce carried a covered casserole dish and a jug of moonshine. She angled her head to see around me. "Hello!" she called to Irina. With her cherub cheeks and tightly coiled gray curls, her quintessential grandma exterior fooled a lot of people into thinking she was harmless. But I'd known her long enough to recognize the twinkle in her warm brown eyes for what it was—trouble.

It was my own fault. I should've waited until Irina was

safely on a flight home before telling Helen and the girls about yesterday's stunt. From the set of Helen's frail shoulders and the bulging pockets of her navy cardigan, she'd come prepared for war.

"Be nice." I warned. "No magic bombs in the house."

Helen huffed and elbowed her way past me. "We'll see about that."

"It's too early for this," I muttered. But I stepped aside because there was no stopping these two when they set their minds on something.

Alyce bustled around the table, making room for her breakfast contributions. I peered over her shoulder as she uncovered the dish. She'd brought Jello salad, her specialty. I grimaced as I tried to identify the floaty bits that looked suspiciously like blobs of scrambled eggs and sausage. Irina turned a little green at the sight but quickly recovered her usual poise.

She smiled graciously as she greeted my witches. "Please join us. I'm Irina Volkov, Maxim's mother."

"Oh, our girl Riley has told us all about you." Helen extended a dainty liver-spotted hand. "I'm Helen." Irina's eyes widened when Helen shook hands like a two-hundred-pound man, her grip firm enough to elicit a wince.

Alyce smiled serenely. "And I'm Alyce. We thought we'd bring over a little something to celebrate your visit."

Helen patted her cardigan pocket.

I quickly set two more places at the table. At least seated, Helen would have a hard time lobbing ants-in-your-pants bombs at Max's mother.

Helen chose the seat directly across from Irina and added a crepe to her plate. "How is your stab wound, hon?" Although the question was for me, Helen stared at Irina as she asked it.

"You know, from when you took a knife meant for the alpha's back."

Irina paled. "Knife?"

"All healed up." I kicked Helen under the table, and she bared her teeth.

"Do you like to garden, Irina?" Helen changed the subject abruptly.

Irina relaxed. "I do. I have a wonderful gardener who is an absolute artist with design."

"How lovely," Helen said conversationally. "Did you know the weather in this area is ideal for growing wolfsbane?" she asked with a sharp smile.

This was going downhill fast.

I reached for the orange juice "Drink?" I offered in an attempt to change the subject.

Alyce slid a crystal glass across the table for Helen and grabbed one for herself. "I have something better." She opened her moonshine and poured a little in her glass, bypassing Helen and me who never touched the stuff. Alyce pointed to Irina's empty glass. "Would you like to try some of my famous moonshine? I've been saving this batch for a special occasion."

I covered Irina's glass with my hand. "It's a bit early for a drink that stout, Alyce. Maybe later." Or never.

Alyce's face was the picture of grandmotherly concern as she watched Irina. "I'm happy to dilute it with orange juice if it's too strong for your delicate stomach."

Helen chortled and bit into her crepe.

Irinia narrowed her eyes. "I'm Russian. I drink vodka like you Americans drink water." She shoved her glass toward Alyce.

Alyce obliged, splashing some moonshine into the glass before setting the jug on the table. Irina smiled, picked up the jug, and poured herself a more generous amount. Then, she clinked it with Alyce's glass before tossing the contents back like a co-ed at Sundowner's half-price shots night.

Alyce's undiluted moonshine was like pouring gasoline down your throat and chasing it with fire. I waited for the coughing fit to start.

Irina's eyes didn't even water. She patted the corner of her mouth with her linen napkin and poured another round.

I gaped at her as she downed the second glass as quickly as she had the first. Then, I confiscated the jug before she could pour a third. Russian or not, that was going to hit hard in fifteen minutes. I hoped her shifter metabolism burned it out of her system before Alyce goaded her into dancing on the table.

"While you're both here, I could use some help," I said.

Helen was still giving Irina the stink eye, but at least she didn't reach for a potion bomb. "What do you need, hon?"

While I'd love to have this conversation without Volkov's mother at the table, I needed a neutral topic. I told them about our progress hunting for the clues, including the final clue which I'd been wearing all along "Do you think you could get access to the Kansas City coven's library?" I had to lock down the artifact before Bellarose or one of the vamps beat me to it.

Helen nodded. "Alona owes me."

"The sooner, the better," I said, hoping it would prod them out the door.

"I'll see what I can dig up." With one last look at Irina, Helen finished her orange juice and stood. "Are you sure you don't want to come with us? We can hit up the coven's smoothie bar."

"Tempting, but I need to finish going through Max's books

this morning. We can meet at headquarters tonight to compare notes. I'll order pizza."

Helen shook a finger at me. "No weird fruit on it this time."

"No pineapple." I crossed my heart before giving them both a hug. "Thank you," I whispered, as much for always having my back as for the research assistance.

CHAPTER 9

*A*fter a day exchanging awkward small talk with Volkov's mother, the last thing I wanted to deal with was the assassin lounging outside headquarters.

"I still don't have the artifact, Sato." I'd given the man an update on the drive home, so unless he thought I discovered the vessel hidden at a rest stop, I wasn't sure why he was here. I shielded the keypad with my body while punching in the security code.

Kage Sato peeled his lanky body from the brick wall and stalked after me. Although we had a betting pool going for what type of supernatural he was, none of us knew for sure. As a man, the notorious Shadow could pass for a Japanese fitness model. He appeared to be an unassuming and, based on the Dungeons & Dragons t-shirt he wore, slightly nerdy twenty-something. Few would guess he was as lethal as he was pretty until they looked into those unsettling dark eyes.

Sato followed me through the door. "You can give me a progress update when we get upstairs."

"But that's not why you came," I guessed.

"Let's save that discussion for upstairs as well."

The first floor of our headquarters had a fully equipped gym and a parking space for our tricked-out van. It also housed a glass-encased office with an armory that saw far more use than the giant laser printer I'd scored from an office liquidation sale. If I hadn't been expecting the rest of my crew to arrive momentarily, I would've shepherded Sato into the sterile office for our chat. Instead, we trekked up four flights of stairs to our team gathering space.

Dez was already sitting at his bank of computers when we arrived upstairs. His ginger head popped up long enough to see who came in before he went back to work.

Sato paused behind Dez to watch the live security feed from the camera aimed at our front door. "You've been up here the whole time I waited, haven't you?"

"Yup." Dez kept typing. He ignored Sato to give me his pizza preferences. "Pepperoni, extra sauce, black olives. No mushrooms." When I didn't answer, he scowled at me. "I'm serious, Riley. I don't want to have to pick off slimy mushrooms this time. They're disgusting." For someone who drank blood, Dez had a lot of food aversions. Of course, he still mixed the blood into tomato juice the way parents hid crushed-up medicine in applesauce for their children, so maybe that shouldn't be surprising.

"Yeah. Yeah. I got it." I added his request along with a variety of other large pizzas and breadsticks before placing the order. "Forty-five minutes."

Dez rolled his eyes. "It always says forty-five minutes. That could mean half an hour or two hours."

I shrugged. He wasn't wrong, but as long as the pizzas stayed hot, I'd take them.

Helen arrived next, followed by Nash and Garth. Helen

immediately scooped Garth up and cooed to him like she hadn't seen him in weeks. Garth preened, accepting the handful of dried black fly larvae she offered as his due.

Janis and Alyce were giving a sewing class tonight at the Stitch Witch and Bea had a pole dancing class, so none of them could join us. Because Irina planned to stay for a week-long visit despite the tension between them, Volkov wouldn't be here either. And Kali and Craig had a hot date planned that trumped an evening buried in magical reference books.

"That's everyone," I told Sato.

"Good. How is the search for Zagan's Chalice progressing?"

Nash crossed his arms over his chest and leaned against the wall, studying Sato as I gave a bare-bones update. I considered telling Sato our theory about the runes being the next clue. As the Enclave's representative, Kage Sato had access to a far more extensive library than we did, which could help us identify those runes. In the end, I kept that information to myself though. If he proved to be our leak, I couldn't risk him deciphering the runes before we did or sharing them with Zara Bellarose. Instead, I told him I had a video call set up with Maria Baca to locate the final clue.

Sato frowned. "You need to speed up the search. We're running out of time. Things have been put in motion that can't be stopped."

I raised a brow. "What kind of things?"

"We have reason to believe others may know about the will," Sato said.

On the surface, his admission made it seem less likely he was our leak. But it could also mean that he knew Bellarose was on our heels because he'd been the one to tell her where we were. Or maybe he simply heard the same rumors swirling about the vampires that Volkov reported.

Before I could ask questions, Sato pinned me with a hard stare. "And the elemental child we had secured has disappeared."

The air left my lungs at the news. This was the first time Sato acknowledged that the Enclave had the child despite my suspicions. "Disappeared?"

"She went missing a week ago from the safe house where we placed her." He continued watching me. "You wouldn't happen to know anything about that, would you?"

I jerked in surprise. "How would I know anything about it? Until now, I wasn't even sure you had the child."

"You've shown a great deal of interest in the child's location," he said. "I don't need to remind you that the child is a key piece to the demon prophecy. In the wrong hands, she will be the tool used to destroy our world."

"She is a child," I bit out, "not some pawn for the Enclave or the demons." I balled my hands into fists at my side, reminded of what it felt like to be a child without agency over my life. "But I had nothing to do with her disappearance." Worry churned in my gut at the idea of her being at the mercy of a vampire loyal to one of the demon kings.

Something dark and predatory rose in Sato's eyes as he watched my reaction. "If I find out you are lying, you will not like the consequences."

Helen and Garth moved toward Sato, but I held up a hand to stop them from attacking. Every instinct in my body urged me to bolt. I forced myself to remain still. "I had nothing to do with her disappearance," I repeated.

After a few seconds, whatever I'd glimpsed inside Sato receded. He stood gracefully from his chair. "Find that artifact, Riley, before someone else gets their hands on it." He left without another word, his warning hanging in the air.

"He's an asshole." Nash broke the tension. "But I don't think he's our leak."

"Agreed." I exhaled. "We need to locate the artifact fast though before the vamps do." Because once they had all the pieces to fulfill the prophecy, they'd use the child to open the veil. And I was certain she wouldn't survive it. "Let's go over what we know, so we can get to work. Dez, did you find anything on Bellarose?"

Dez pushed his glasses up the bridge of his nose and rolled his office chair out from behind his wall of monitors. "She's overhauled her security system. All her cameras are local only, so I can't hack them unless I'm on the ground. But I did get into all the nearby security systems and traffic cams."

He spun one of the monitors around so we could see it. The feed was from across the street with a clear view of the front of Bellarose's building. Two armed guards stood next to the entry door. Another guard patrolled the perimeter, disappearing around the side of the building.

Dez pointed to the guards. "They're on a regular rotation. But that's not the most interesting part." He zoomed in on the top floor where all the windows were blacked out with steel shutters. "She's also stepped-up physical security since we hit her penthouse."

Nash whistled. "She must be spooked to go to such extremes to keep intruders out."

When we'd broken in, she'd already had bars that could be activated with a button to block the exits. That's why I had to go through the front door to escape. But steel shutters were an upgrade. "What about inside?" I asked Dez. "Does she have guards in the building?"

"Yeah," Dez said. "Two guards go inside every time there's a shift change."

Helen grinned at me. "I bet she upped her wards, too. Not that those could do diddly to keep you out."

"And she's there?" I asked.

Dez nodded. "She hasn't left since returning from New Mexico with her bodyguards in tow."

"Good. Keep tabs on her. We need to know when she leaves and where she goes."

"Lucky for us, all her vehicles are outfitted with GPS," Dez said. "Unless she disables the navigation on all of them, I'll be able to track her."

I turned to Nash. "That reminds me. Did you ever find the bug on your truck?" We needed to be certain that's how she'd been tracking us.

"Volkov said Arlo found and disabled it."

Dez stiffened. "Arlo?"

I cringed and glared at Nash, who shrugged. "Arlo is the one who drove the truck back to Kansas City. I knew you'd be salty about it, so I didn't tell you."

"Whatever." He rolled his chair behind the monitors again. "I checked your phones, and they're clear." Dez's lip curled as he tossed a phone to Nash. "Unless you already knew that because Arlo told you."

"Great." I took my phone out of Dez's hand before he could throw it and ignored his Arlo dig. "At least we know how Bellarose was tracking us. Let's sweep all our vehicles regularly."

Everyone murmured their agreement.

I held my ring up and tapped the runes. "That leaves figuring out what these mean."

"We've looked through every book on runes we can get

our hands on," Helen said. "We can't find anything that matches."

I'd had no better luck going through Volkov's library.

Garth pecked Helen's pant leg to get her attention before waddling over to the bookcase where we'd stashed his Ouija board.

Helen grabbed the board and sat it on the floor. "Garth, do you recognize those runes?"

The rooster bobbed his head. We all crowded closer as he moved the planchette across the surface to spell out his answer—demon runes. When Helen read it out loud, Garth crowed before grooming his feathers.

I stared at the silver and copper ring my mother left for me. "That can't be good." Why would my human mother even know what a demon rune was, much less use them?

Garth attacked my leg.

"Ouch. What was that for?"

He marched back to the Ouija board. This time, he spelled out the word reveal.

"Reveal what?" I asked.

Garth clucked and nudged the planchette again. "Secret."

Nash frowned. "What the hell is that supposed to mean?"

Garth lost interest in the Ouija board and clucked, demanding a treat for his efforts.

"Good boy." Helen petted Garth before tossing a few treats on the ground. She studied me thoughtfully. "With any other kind of rune, you'd short circuit the magic. Your mom must have known that. But even demon runes have to be activated."

"By blood?" Dez guessed.

"Possibly," Helen said.

"These weren't activated by blood." I took the ring off my finger and held it up to the light, examining the small tick marks on the inside. "These marks didn't appear until I borrowed Phoebe Thompson's magic. That was the trigger. And the runes aren't the clue. The marks are."

I handed the ring to Dez. "Can you zoom in on the marks and project the image on a screen?"

"Sure."

A few seconds later, the image was big enough that we could see they weren't tick marks at all.

"Well, I'll be damned." Nash pointed to the numbers on the screen. "Those are coordinates."

My pulse sped up, and I leaned closer to the monitor. "To where?"

We collectively held our breath as Dez opened maps and typed in the coordinates. I expected him to pull up an address in New Mexico.

Nash scratched his bearded cheek. "Your mom didn't want to make this easy, did she?"

"Doesn't seem so," I agreed. The location wasn't in New Mexico. "Looks like we're going to need a plane."

Dez zoomed in on the remote island off the coast of Norway. "And a boat."

CHAPTER 10

hanks to a rich boyfriend with access to a jet, Nash, Dez, and I were on the ground in Florø, Norway two days later. The private flight kept our names off any reservations that Zara Bellarose—or other interested parties —could track. Since landing in Norway yesterday afternoon, Nash had triple-scouted the area. He hadn't spotted anyone suspicious, only friendly locals willing to share recommendations for good food and gorgeous day trips. Last night, we'd watched Bellarose enter her Toronto penthouse via the street-view security feed Dez hacked into, ensuring she was far from Norway.

Yet, there was an itch on the nape of my neck setting me on edge. After dodging Bellarose for days in New Mexico, Nash and I both were diligent about watching for tails. When neither of us discovered any, I chalked my nerves up to anticipation for our coming scavenger hunt and focused on preparing for today's excursion.

Arranging accommodations in the western coastal town of Florø yesterday had been easy enough. Finding a charter boat willing to shuttle us to an uninhabited island and then return at an undetermined day and time took more legwork. After asking around and negotiating a generous fee, Dez arranged for a ride to meet us in an hour.

While Nash and I traveled to the small island off the coast, Dez would remain at our charming two-bedroom vacation rental. Dez had already transformed one bedroom into a makeshift command center, complete with several monitors and an assortment of gadgets he'd insisted on packing. From here, Dez could monitor Bellarose's location as well as watch the satellites he'd hijacked to let us know if anyone else headed to the island. The last thing I wanted was to get my hands on that artifact only to have someone swoop in and take it from me. Dez was our early alert system.

From the satellite imagery, the only inhabitants on the island itself appeared to be birds, small mammals, and a herd of wild goats that roamed the mountains. Other than an abandoned shack near the coast that had probably been used by fishermen, there wasn't any infrastructure, which meant we'd be roughing it. On the bright side, it also meant the only adversary we'd likely face was the weather, which so far had been a reasonable forty degrees with blue skies.

I held up the phone Dez handed me as we packed the last of our supplies. "You're sure this will work out there?"

"It's a sat phone, Riley. It should work everywhere on the island," Dez assured me.

"Alright." I zipped the phone into the front compartment of my backpack.

Nash tossed me the food packets he'd brought along. I made a face but added them to my stash. Next time Nash and I went off grid, I really needed to source the camping food myself, so I wasn't stuck eating freeze-dried beans. We were also bringing water bottles in addition to a couple life straws we could use to filter water sources if our search kept us on the island longer than a day. Neither of us was wasting packing space on extra clothes. While I stuffed food and water, first aid supplies, an emergency blanket, and climbing gear into my pack, Nash loaded his with an assortment of weapons from blades to explosives.

"What?" Nash asked when he caught both Dez and I staring at him.

Dez shook his head. "You got a real Rambo fetish, don't you?"

"Better than a Poindexter fetish," Nash shot back.

A day spent crammed in a plane and then a vacation rental meant the two of them had regressed to bickering like siblings.

"Poindexter was a book nerd." Dez pointed to his stash of computer equipment. "If you would've said Linus Torvalds, your insult would actually make sense."

I squinted at Dez. "Who?"

Seeing the blank looks on both our faces, Dez sighed. "Never mind."

Nash nodded toward my full pack. "That everything?"

"Yup." I threaded my arms through the straps and adjusted it on my back. "Now, let's go get that artifact."

By the time the chartered boat neared our drop off, the weather had turned rainy, the clouds reducing visibility. I held my breath as the island came into view, rising like paradise from the rough waters surrounding it. Most of the terrain was steep and rugged and the surrounding waters shallow, which left few places for a boat to dock. Our ride dropped us as close to the coast as he dared go. From there, we traveled by kayak.

We soon landed on the side of the island with the fishing

shack. Even in March, the island vegetation was greening up in the grassy meadow below the mountains. There were few signs of visitors save the dilapidated shack up ahead. Because it was the only standing structure, we checked it out first, leaving our kayaks next to it.

The one-room building was clad in weathered-ravaged wood, the windows long since broken. Inside housed a single bunk without a mattress, a small table, and a bin holding a camping plate, dusty utensils, and an ancient can of unopened tuna. Nothing in or around the shack sparked a memory, so after checking the floorboards and testing the walls for hidden compartments, Nash and I stepped outside.

Nash adjusted his pack and surveyed the coastline. "Anything familiar so far?"

"No." I pointed to an overgrown trail leading further inland. "That seems like our best route up the mountain."

I scanned the areas as we walked, relishing the crisp spring air and the virgin wilderness around us. Kansas had plenty of wide, open spaces, but this island was peaceful in a way that populated areas could never achieve.

Ahead of me, Nash bent to examine the trail, noting faint tracks. "Looks like only animals have used this for quite some time."

"Good. That means it's less likely someone beat us to the demon artifact." I edged past Nash and picked up the pace. Before long, the trail sloped upward, the incline becoming steeper with every step. "Doing okay back there?" I called over my shoulder.

Nash chuckled. "Don't worry about me, kiddo. I'll keep up."

The further inland we hiked, the more alert I became, my ears listening for the snap of a twig or a heavy footfall. I heard nothing beyond the whistle of the wind and the occasional bird call. But I couldn't shake the uneasy feeling that we were being watched. "Are you getting the sense we're not alone?" I asked Nash under my breath. I chanced a look behind me in time to see Nash unzip his jacket.

When he noticed me looking, he patted the gun he wore in a shoulder holster and cut his eyes to the right. "Four o'clock," he mouthed. "Keep moving. I'll catch up."

I spun around, purposely making my steps heavy as we rounded the next bend. I didn't have to look behind me to know that Nash peeled away to circle behind whoever was following us. A few seconds later, I heard something crash through the underbrush. When Nash reappeared, he had the culprit firmly in hand.

I grinned. "That is not who I was expecting."

"That makes two of us." Nash scowled at me, as he pinned the wild goat to his side.

The goat was not happy about being manhandled, bucking and twisting in Nash's grip. "Why do you have him by the horns, anyway?" I asked.

"Because he head butted me twice," Nash growled.

Not one to back down, the goat spit-yelled and attempted a repeat performance.

While Nash wrestled the wild goat, I crossed my arms over my chest, taking in the show. "When you think about it, me letting all those goats out in your yard when we met prepared you for this. You're welcome," I teased. Dez and I had dumped a van full of goats on Nash's doorstep as a diversion tactic, so that I could break into his house and steal a demon dagger. I grinned remembering the chaos.

"Yeah right." Nash twisted the goat's head until his horns were aimed in the opposite direction.

"You know the second you let go, he's going to nail you, right?"

"Really helpful, Riley."

I moved closer to lend a hand but stilled when movement caught my eye. I scanned the vegetation on both sides of us. Unease tickled the back of my neck, and I sucked in a breath when I glimpsed eyes watching from the trees.

"We have company." I pulled my dagger and dropped into a fighter's stance. I didn't have long to wait.

"You've got to be shitting me." Nash shoved the goat away from him, swatting it on the rump. Unruffled, the goat head butted Nash again before joining the rest of the herd now surrounding us. From the way they were lowering their horns, they weren't petting zoo friendly. "Any bright ideas?" Nash asked.

"One." I tucked my dagger and my mother's ring into my backpack and started to strip.

CHAPTER 11

$\mathcal{A}$s I shifted, I prepared myself for the dominance battle sure to come. But the second I stood on four legs instead of two, the herd's aggression turned into something else. The goats closed ranks, brushing up against my sides as if offering comfort. One of the younger goats jumped sideways, her joy contagious. Several others joined her. Even the goat that had been stubbornly attacking Nash lowered his head and rubbed his face against mine.

Nash massaged his thigh where he'd been clipped by a horn, watching as the herd went from hostile to downright cuddly. "Looks like you've got a fan club, kiddo." He grabbed my backpack from the ground and stuffed my abandoned clothes inside. "For both our sakes, I think you should stay in goat form for a while."

I bleated my agreement. When I headed down the same path we'd been traveling though, several of the herd blocked the way while others nudged me off the trail. Despite several attempts to return to the path, our escorts refused to allow us passage.

Like most animals, goats were instinct-driven creatures. If they were this determined to lead me away from the well-worn trail, I figured there was a good chance danger awaited us in that direction. I tapped Nash's hip with my horns before crashing through the underbrush with my newfound friends. Although Nash cursed under his breath, he followed our lead.

Half an hour of climbing later, I stopped so abruptly, Nash nearly tripped over me.

"What is it?" He kept his voice low as he scanned the clearing up ahead.

I shifted to human. The buzz of magic hung thick in the air, and goosebumps broke out all over my skin. "Lots and lots of wards." I stared at the crisscrossed threads as I dressed.

I'd never seen anything like it. Usually, wards were set around a perimeter of a building or across entry points. Occasionally, stronger witches layered them, with some keyed to prevent supernaturals from entering and others set to bar humans. But I'd never encountered a dome like this that was designed to keep out intruders from both land and sky.

Each ward was a distinct color, woven together to form a giant dome. There were so many that I could only glimpse the trees and buildings beyond the magic. The massive size, spanning more than a city block, must have taken weeks to construct. Someone went to a lot of trouble to protect whatever was under that dome. The frayed patches of the weave indicated whoever set the wards did so a long time ago.

"That must mean the artifact is here." Nash followed my gaze, his brows pinched when he couldn't see the kaleidoscope of magic I saw. "Can we get through them?"

"That depends." The man's deep voice made us both jump.

I'd been so focused on the wards, I hadn't noticed that I wasn't the only one who'd shifted to human. With shaggy blonde hair and an athletic build, the man appeared to be in his early thirties. From the proud tilt of his head and the steady eye contact, the man now standing on two legs was the one responsible for the gouge in Nash's thigh.

The others took longer to shift as the pop and crack of bones realigning soon filled the clearing. In the twenty-five years I'd been alive, I couldn't recall ever encountering another goat shifter. Now, I stood surrounded by the half-shifted bodies of a dozen people like me. A sense of belonging swelled in my chest, clogging my throat and stealing my voice while I watched horns recede into smooth foreheads and hooves become feet.

The man who spoke didn't wait for the others. I tried not to stare at his naked ass when he strode past us toward the dome.

Nash recovered from the shock faster than I did. "Depends on what?" he asked.

The man glanced at us. "On whether you're a witch." Then, he passed through the wards like they weren't even there.

I frowned. Technically, I was as much a witch as I was a shifter. Since I hadn't met a ward that could keep me out yet, I squared my shoulders and took my chances. The magic welcomed me like an old friend, curving around my body and humming against my skin. I turned in time to see Nash put his shoulder down and barrel through. When he encountered only air, he staggered but kept his feet under him.

I laughed. "You know it's magic, right? You can't break it down like a door."

Nash shrugged. "How the hell would I know how to bust through a ward?" Like the soldier he was trained to be, he was already assessing the area for danger.

Small cottages were arranged in a circle inside the dome,

with another row of homes inside the outer ring. In the center, a large communal space filled the clearing including rough-hewn picnic tables, an outdoor grill, and a food prep area on one side. The remainder of the space was dedicated to recreation tailor-made for goats with an elaborate series of platforms and ramps perfect for climbing and jumping.

The man we'd followed through the wards intercepted us before we could explore. At least he'd donned a pair of loose-fitting cotton pants, so we weren't facing a full-frontal view. "No weapons beyond this point." He held out a hand to Nash as the others crowded around us.

Nash scowled but relinquished his gun. When the man kept staring at him expectantly, he added two knives to the pile and then a set of brass knuckles.

"Your backpacks, too," the man insisted as he patted Nash down to ensure no weapons made it past him.

I tossed mine next to Nash's arsenal, wishing I'd had the foresight to smuggle my dagger beneath my clothes rather than putting it inside my backpack. At least I still had the small pocketknife I carried in my jacket. No one searched me. One advantage of being a willowy pink-haired woman was that, unlike Nash, few people expected me to be armed.

After confiscating our weapons, the man gestured for us to follow him. "Come."

Nash planted his feet and crossed his arms. "Where are you taking us?"

The man kept walking. "To meet with one of our elders, who will decide what to do with you."

Well, that didn't sound ominous at all.

Nash and I exchanged a worried look before following him through the village. Smoke curled from the steep roofs of small wood cabins, drifting through the patchwork magic forming the dome above us. Several residents dressed in homespun clothing ambled out of their cottages and stopped what they were doing to stare.

With so many eyes on us, Nash tensed, automatically reaching for the reassurance of his weapons. "Keep your guard up." His hand clenched at the reminder he was unarmed.

The villagers seemed more curious than hostile as they watched us pass their homes though. In the center of the village, a group of children ignored us completely, their full attention on stealing the ball they kicked amongst them. Up ahead, a burly man with a bushy beard and hard eyes stepped into our path. Unlike the others, there was no curiosity in his perusal.

He pointed a finger at us as he confronted our escort. "They shouldn't be here," he rumbled. "They don't belong."

"That's not for you to decide." Our guide didn't break stride, moving to go around him. When the roadblock moved to intercept him, our escort lowered his forehead as if he still had horns in human form. "Step aside, Jakob, or I'll make you."

After a few tense seconds, he moved to the side, his jaw clenched. Nash walked ahead of me, shoulder-checking the man in warning as he passed. As soon as Nash was clear, the man narrowed the path again, his body so close I smelled the fish on his breath as I edged past him. His hand clamped onto my bicep so quickly I couldn't avoid it as he yanked me to a halt. His bone-crushing grip tightened. "I know what you are, girl, and I'll be watching you," he snarled, looming over me.

Terror made my heart stutter in my chest. For a second, I was a teen back in Santa Fe, Tony's hand on my arm and his vile suggestions in my ear as I tried to survive a pack that hated me. I trembled, and this man's smile turned vicious.

His eyes widened as I stepped into his body, no doubt expecting me to attempt to break free. But I'd spent too many years fending off angry hands to waste time on a power struggle I'd never win. Instead, I bent my elbow and gripped his forearm. Then, I punched him in the face, twisted my body, and hammered my other elbow against his arm to break his hold. Before I let go, I drove my knee into his lower back.

I put distance between us before pulling my switchblade from my jacket pocket and flicking it open. "You ever put your hands on me again, and I'll bury this in your gut."

The confrontation happened so fast that the two men in front of us barely had time to react. By the time Nash and our escort noticed, several villagers had formed a semi-circle around us. I waited for the ugly words and hurled insults. But none of their outrage was directed at me. Unlike my old pack that had been happy to look the other way as dominant wolves terrorized weaker pack members, these villagers seemed angry on my behalf. They berated my attacker even as our guide warned him to stay far away from me.

Nash forced his way through the crowd to get to me. "You okay?"

The adrenaline still crashing through my system made it difficult to speak, so I nodded. Nash took the switchblade from my shaky fingers and closed it, tucking it into my jacket pocket. For the rest of the walk, he hovered like a bodyguard, sending dark looks at anyone who got close to me.

When I finally stopped shaking, he nudged me with an elbow. "Nice uppercut."

"Thanks. I've been practicing." All those sparring sessions at headquarters paid off.

Our escort stopped in front of a small cabin with a rustic rocking chair on its porch. He turned to face us, blocking the door with his body, but he didn't demand I turn over my knife. "Olav is an old man recovering from pneumonia. Do not upset him."

I frowned. "We have no intention of upsetting anyone." No one except the bully I'd just dropped with a well-placed knee, anyway.

Satisfied with my answer, he knocked twice. It took several minutes for the door to open. The elder who greeted us was stooped with age and wheezing from his bout of pneumonia, but his bright blue eyes were sharp as they took in my rumpled clothes and pink hair. He clutched his chest and met my gaze. For a second, I feared the shock of strangers at his door was too much.

But he pushed our guide out of the way and touched my cheek. "You look so much like Henrik." Grief choked his voice, and he blinked away tears.

The sounds of the village faded into white noise, and my pulse thudded in my ears. "Who's Henrik?" I whispered.

"My son. And your father."

CHAPTER 12

*E*ven when DNA results proved Amelia wasn't my biological mother, I'd stubbornly clung to the hope that Santiago and I had been bound with blood. And yet, the truth was in the hue of Olav's bright blue eyes—so like my own—in the angle of his nose and the arch of his brows. Olav and I stood on the threshold of his home, tangled together in the joy and sorrow of this moment as we took stock of one another.

Despite being in his early seventies and recovering from illness, Olav held himself with a quiet dignity that demanded respect. When the man who brought us to his door offered to supervise our visit, one withering look from Olav sent him scurrying away, leaving Nash and me alone with my grandfather.

Inside, we stepped into a main living area with two doors leading to what I assumed were a bedroom and bathroom. The walls were exposed wood, with amateur watercolor paintings hanging in rustic frames. Olav's simple home held plenty of soft touches—a patchwork quilt across the back of a well-worn couch, a framed cross-stitch of a lighthouse, and a row of delicate teacups hanging from a rail in the kitchen nook.

When he noticed what drew my attention, Olav smiled. "Mementos from your grandmother, Stella. She's been gone for thirty years." He reached for my hands, holding them with the strength honed from a life without excess conveniences. "What is your name, child?"

"It's Riley Cruz."

Olav's smile faltered at hearing my last name, but he recovered quickly. "You kept your first name then. That's good."

So many questions bubbled up, but I asked the easiest one first. "What's your last name?"

"Larsen. In the beginning, it was your name, too." Seeing how I nervously twisted my fingers together to keep the overwhelming emotions at bay, Olav's tone lightened. "Now then, let me see you, child." He studied me before tugging a strand of my pink hair with a grin. "You have a wild streak like your father."

"Yes, she does," Nash agreed and introduced himself.

"Come." Olav gestured to a wooden dining room chair across from the couch for Nash.

Once I settled on the couch, Olav joined me. "I knew one day you'd return home," he said.

"How did you know it was me?" While we shared a family resemblance, Olav recognized me the instant he'd opened his door.

"You crossed our wards." He propped an embroidered pillow behind his lower back before turning to me. "They were set to keep witches and other supernaturals out. But our herd is immune to magic."

I sucked in a breath. I'd never heard of anyone other than me who was resistant to magic. It made sense though that it would be an inherited trait. "All of you are unaffected by magic?"

"Most magic, yes."

I nodded, understanding our limitations. I'd already discovered demon magic could still affect me. Even elemental magic could be used against me in some instances. Being immune to the magic itself didn't prevent water from drowning me or a blast of air from smashing objects into my body.

Nash leaned forward in his chair. "You can resist shifter commands and vampire compulsions like Riley as well?"

Olav winked at me. "No one tells a goat what to do."

Both Nash and I smiled.

I thought about the warded dome sheltering this village and of the rarity of goat shifters in the broader world. "So, your village is cut off from the rest of the supernatural community?" I wondered if the Enclave left them alone. If so, this little island was paradise indeed.

Olav took a deep breath, the air rattling through his lungs. "We keep to ourselves. More so now than we used to." He gestured toward the door. "The world out there is full of rules and enemies we want no part of."

It appeared the aversion to rules was genetic as well.

I gathered my courage and asked what I most wanted to know. "Will you tell me about my parents? What were they like?" I ignored the twinge of guilt I felt at calling anyone other than Santiago and Amelia Cruz my parents.

Olav reached for a framed photograph lying face-down on the table. When he caught my curious look, he cleared his throat. "Some days, the reminder is too hard."

I nodded because I understood the sharp edge of grief all too well.

Olav traced a finger across the glass before handing the photograph to me. "Your father was the life of every party." He smiled softly. "Even as a baby, he laughed more than he cried."

The photo showed a young Henrik, the lanky teen's wild mop of brown curls and his thousand-watt smile at odds with the serious expression of the man next to him. I pointed to the older man. "Is this you?"

Olav smiled. "Yes. Henrik insisted we get that picture taken at a photo booth in Bergen when we visited. We traveled to the bigger cities once a year to get supplies, sell our goods, and experience the wider world." A glimmer of pain clouded his eyes as he gazed down at the framed photo in my hands. "I thought the photo booth was a waste of money, so he paid for the picture himself. Now, it is my most treasured possession."

I spun my mother's ring on my finger before guiding the conversation to happier ground. "So, Henrik was fun-loving?"

"That he was." Olav's shoulders slumped against the thread-bare couch. "But his zest for life sometimes made him chase the wrong things."

I scooted closer to him. "What kind of things?" I stared down at the smiling face of the young man who would later become my father, and I imagined him courting danger the way I often did. Did Henrik embrace the adrenaline rush that came from a heart-pounding jump, a high-speed race, or the thrill of a heist like I did? Was that where I got it?

"Like your mother," Olav said.

I winced at the flash of anger on Olav's face. "My mother?"

Olav used the couch arm to hoist himself to his feet. "What kind of host am I? I should offer you refreshments after your journey." He shuffled into his tidy kitchen, banging cabinet doors as he avoided my gaze. Several minutes later, he returned with a plate of homemade shortbread cookies and mismatched glasses filled with cold water for the three of us. When I opened my mouth to ask again about my mother, Olav thrust a cookie into my hand. "Eat first. Then, I will tell you what you need to know."

I choked down a cookie, following it with a swig of my water before turning expectantly toward Olav.

He cleared his throat but didn't avoid the topic this time. "The summer Henrik turned twenty-one, he spent three months in Oslo. Back then, we were not as insulated as we are now, and it was customary for our young people to spend a season traveling and experiencing the world. Some even attended universities to study or learn a trade, but my Henrik didn't have the patience to sit idle in a classroom. He found a job on a fishing boat that paid enough to rent a room." Olav shook his head. "I visited him once. Everything smelled like fish—his clothes, his hair. Saltwater even clung to the walls in that place. But he was happy there." He took a drink of his water when his voice grew shaky. "That's where he met your mother. She was young and ambitious, and she snared him with a sweet face and empty praise. He brought her to the island, even though she was an outsider and not a shifter like us." Olav grimaced. "He couldn't see past the mask she wore like the rest of us could. The more we warned him that she was not good for him, the tighter he clung to her. And then you came." He reached for my hand again, holding it gently like a treasure. "You inherited her dark blonde hair, Henrik's eyes, and my lungs." He chuckled. "The whole village heard you when you were hungry."

Nash laughed with my grandfather. "Some things never change," he teased.

I rolled my eyes and grabbed another cookie, hanging on to every crumb of Olav's story. "Were they happy?"

"For a bit," Olav conceded. "But Rosa—that was your mother's name—wanted to leave this place, move to somewhere bigger." Olav's gaze dropped to his lap, and shame tinged his voice. "I told Henrik if he left, he could not come back. As one of ours, I insisted you belonged here and forbid them from taking you from the island." He held up a trembling hand with a rueful smile. "Hard to believe this of an old man, but I was the strongest buck then, and the villagers were easily swayed to my side. They had never warmed to Rosa, seeing her still as an outsider."

I thought back to the words Jakob hurled at me, the distrust and hatred he aimed at a stranger among them. For a new mother, to have everyone except her mate reject her must've been horrible. Maybe it wasn't as bad as living in Carl's pack, but it would've been lonely just the same. Despite the regret Olav wore plainly, I couldn't help the anger that welled up on her behalf. "You forced them to stay with people who hated her," I accused.

Olav sighed. "They didn't hate her, but they feared her. At first because we were afraid she'd keep Henrik and you from us."

As I watched the play of emotions on Olav's lined face, my palms grew clammy, sensing that wasn't the worst of it. "And later?"

"And later, they feared her power. Rosa grew increasingly agitated when Henrik refused to leave with her. She barricaded the two of you in the little cottage they shared, barring your father from entering. When Henrik finally forced his way into their home weeks later, he found you distraught and Rosa unkept, muttering about destiny. She'd stocked their kitchen with potions and filled their home with ominous writings."

My stomach cramped and my mind raced with the nagging suspicion I didn't want to acknowledge.

Nash pushed for the answers I dreaded. "What did she do?"

"She tried to leave with Riley in the middle of the night, but some villagers intercepted her before she could make it to the boats." Olav dropped his head into his hands, his voice thick with grief again. "Henrik's friend Jakob found his body in their home. Poisoned and stabbed in the chest with a kitchen knife. He'd been dead for days, while she'd gathered supplies and plotted her escape."

I wrapped my arms around Olav, offering what little comfort I could, even as my own heart split open in my chest. "I'm so sorry."

He patted my hands. "It is not your fault, child."

I knew he was right. That did nothing to stop the guilt I carried at being the epicenter of the deaths of so many people who'd loved me, who'd attempted to shelter me.

"In the chaos, Rosa escaped. Thankfully, the villagers kept her from taking you with her," Olav said. "For the next two years, she tried to come back for you. But we paid a coven to ward the village against her entry, against all supernaturals except for our herd, to be safe."

"The dome," Nash said.

"Yes," Olav confirmed. "Despite three witches casting those wards, Rosa was powerful enough to crack them, given enough time. But she was impatient." He shifted in his seat so he could meet my eyes. "That's when she sent in the human thief to steal you."

The words hit like a blow, doubling me over. "No." It couldn't be true. "You're wrong. My mother—Amelia Cruz—was hired to find a demon artifact called Zagan's chalice." Olav had to be mistaken. Maybe the loss of his son made him see everything as a threat to me, but even Sato had confirmed the artifact was Amelia's target.

Olav nodded. "That was what she believed as well until she landed on the island. The Shadow who came with her gave her a secondary target and directions to bring down the wards. Until she laid eyes on you, Amelia had no idea she'd been sent to steal a child."

I put my head between my knees and breathed, trying to come to grips with that news. When Olav stroked a tentative hand across my shoulders, I shrugged him off. "No." I sat up. "If that were true, Amelia would've handed me over to Rosa. But she didn't. She kept me, raised me as her own."

Olav pressed his wrinkled hands against his knees as if to stop himself from reaching for me again. "I know." He exhaled, looking at the photo of Henrik he'd returned to its place. "That's because I asked her to."

The front door crashed against the wall, Jakob's towering body filling the frame. "Another boat docked off the coast." His blazing eyes swung to me, the accusation that I'd brought this trouble clear in his expression. "Four people in masks and tactical gear are rowing to shore."

Nash was on his feet, a hand wrapped around my arm before Jakob could say more. "We need to go now."

"He's right." Olav stood and hustled over to a rolling desk, retrieving a sheet of paper and a pencil. He quickly sketched a rough map. "Here." He tapped the X he'd marked. "This is where you'll find answers. The people you knew to be your parents came back years later to bury things in an old vault carved into the mountain. Amelia said you would come here one day needing whatever they put inside."

If my dad came to this island with her, it meant Amelia must've confided in him about her past. I didn't know whether to be relieved she'd trusted him with her secrets or hurt that neither of them told me. I may have been a child when I lost them, but twelve was old enough that they could've prepared me themselves rather than broadside me now.

Olav handed me the map. "Amelia said to tell you to mind the symbols, that your dad," he almost choked on the last word, "that he taught you how to climb the treacherous trail and navigate the traps they laid to keep others out."

I accepted the map but then threw my arms around this stooped man who was the only blood relation I had left. "I don't want to leave," I whispered. "I just found you."

Olav gave me a quick hug. "I'll be right here when you come back, child." He nudged me toward the door. "Now, go get your answers."

CHAPTER 13

Our first stop was to retrieve our weapons. The same group of villagers who had led us to the village earlier gathered near the dome to intercept the newcomers. We watched as they quickly shifted into their goats before venturing beyond the wards. Anyone seeing them would assume, like we had, that they were nothing more than the wild herd rumored to be on this island. When they were gone, Nash holstered his gun and retrieved his knives, while I dug through my backpack for my ringing sat phone.

"Hey—"

Dez cut me off. "What the hell, Riley? Twenty-eight times I tried to call you."

I cringed. "Sorry. Our backpacks, including the phone, were confiscated."

"What do you mean confiscated?" All the anger bled from Dez's tone. "Are you safe?"

Tucking the phone against my shoulder, I strapped on my dagger. After my run-in with Jakob earlier, I wasn't about to travel unarmed. "We're fine. Long story, but it wasn't whoever is headed to the island now."

"So, you saw them?" Dez asked.

"Someone here spotted them and warned us." Before Dez could launch into questions about the island we'd believed to be uninhabited, I got to the point. "Vamps?"

"That'd be my guess. The satellite imagery is grainy, but I count four people coming ashore. From the head-to-toe tactical gear, I'd say they're either paramilitary or sun-shy vamps." Sunlight might not kill vampires like in the movies, but that didn't mean they wanted to spend time exposed to it. "Plus," Dez said, "I checked the feed outside Bellarose's penthouse. She went inside a couple hours ago with a guest and a bodyguard. She hasn't come out since."

"Who's the guest?"

"No clue. By the height, I'd guess a woman, but whoever it was wore a hooded cape."

Not wanting to get into the full story now, I kept it brief. "Nash and I are headed to the location where my mom stashed the artifact. Keep us updated on our party crashers' location."

"That'll be easier if you keep your phone on you this time," Dez grumbled.

"I'll do my best." After tucking the phone into the front pocket, I adjusted my backpack and stepped through the magic. I glanced at the tattered dome as Nash came through. Hopefully, the group landing on the island weren't humans, or they'd be able to walk through as easily as Nash did. Even if they breached the village's wards, I suspected my grandfather would do his best to stall them, giving us as much time as he could to beat them to the underground vault.

Nash and I hiked in silence. I checked the crude map

several times to make sure we were on track. According to Olav's drawing, the trailhead was behind an outcropping of rocks that I hoped were the ones up ahead.

I refolded the map and tucked it into my pocket before pointing to the rocks. "This has to be it."

The trail we found ourselves on was so overgrown that we had to pick our way carefully or risk a sprained ankle. While Nash obscured our trail to slow down any followers, I replayed every shock Olav dealt me. As soon as I had the artifact secured, I planned to sneak into the village and continue our conversation. The longer I walked, the more questions rattled around in my head.

A few minutes later, Nash caught up to me. "You want to talk about it?"

"Not really," I mumbled.

Nash didn't let it go so easily. "You've got to be thinking it, too," he said, side-eyeing me as we kept moving. "Rosa."

I clenched my jaw. "Don't say it. I'm not ready to face it yet."

Maybe if I didn't voice the suspicion out loud, it wouldn't be true. I wanted Amelia Cruz to be my mother, not some deranged woman who had killed her own mate to get to me. And if Rosa ended up being who I feared, it would be unbearable. Normally, I wasn't a woman who bought into coincidences, but I desperately wanted this to be one. The alternative was admitting that Rosa sounded a lot like a nickname for a certain witch.

I stared at the faint trail ahead of us. "Let's worry about getting the artifact, and we can deal with the family drama later."

"Fine. We won't talk about it. Yet." Nash lifted a fallen branch blocking our path and drug it off to the side while changing the subject. "What did Olav mean when he said your dad trained you?"

I shrugged. "No idea. Santiago was the fun dad. Other than teaching me a couple self-defense tricks and showing me meditation exercises to get me to sit still occasionally, he wasn't the training type." Even as I said it, something Olav said dredged up a memory. "Wait. Olav said to mind the symbols."

Nash brushed his hands off on his pants and rejoined me on the path. "You know what symbols he was talking about?"

"Maybe. My dad loved games. When I was a kid, he made these cards. Each one had a symbol on it that represented a game or activity. He'd have me draw one from the pile on weekends to decide what we did." I felt a pang of nostalgia for the fun-filled Saturdays and lazy Sunday mornings I spent with my dad in the backyard of our little rental house in Santa Fe. Most of the other dads in our neighborhood would rather drink beer in their yards with their buddies than spend time playing with their kids. But I was always my dad's first choice. He made sure all my weekends were filled with laughter and adventure.

"And you think those are the symbols he meant?" Nash asked. "For games?"

I checked Olav's map again, noting the gnarled tree off to our right. We were almost to the stretch Olav had labeled as the gauntlet. "I guess we're about to find out."

It didn't take long to stumble across the first symbol. "There." I pointed to a boulder blocking the trail. Three stacked boxes were carved into the rock.

Nash frowned at it. "I hope that doesn't mean we're stacking rocks like building blocks."

"No. It's hopscotch."

"Huh?"

I used a stick to draw the board in the dirt exactly like my dad used to. Then, I demonstrated by hopping on two legs, then one and one, then two again, then one.

Nash grimaced, patting his shoulder holster like he'd rather shoot something than be forced to play hopscotch.

"Come on. It's fun." I showed him again.

Nash grunted but did it. Not gracefully, but he did it. He used the toe of his boot to erase the board. "So what? We're supposed to hop along the trail like fucking rabbits?"

When he said it like that, it sounded pretty stupid. But I recognized that symbol. I climbed on top of the boulder, angling to see what was on the other side. "It's the pattern." I reached down and offered Nash a hand up. Once he sat next to me, I pointed to rough-hewn pavers laid two across and five deep. They took up the full width of the trail, with steep banks on either side. I grinned. "See. Hopscotch."

I slid off the other side of the boulder and waited for Nash. "I'll go first." I tightened the straps on my pack and hopped across, giving him two thumbs up when I stood on the other side. "Your turn. Two, left, left, two, right," I reminded him.

Nash repeated the pattern, then awkwardly hopped his way across.

"You did it!" I held up my hand for a high five. When he ignored it, I grabbed his hand and held it up, so I could slap it.

Nash reached down and grabbed a rock the size of his fist.

"What are you doing?"

"Finding out what would've happened if we got it wrong." He pitched the rock onto a paver that didn't match the pattern. A loud creak echoed through the valley as all ten pavers tilted to one side. With no guardrails or footholds, we would've careened to our death had we been standing on it. A minute later the path righted itself.

"That was a death trap alright," Nash said.

I elbowed him. "Come on. Race you to the next one."

"Riley," he growled.

I smothered a smile. "Kidding."

From there, the climb got steeper and the trail more treacherous. The air thinned as we climbed for another hour. Although we both scanned our surroundings constantly, we didn't come across another symbol. "Maybe that was the only one," I guessed.

Nash laughed. "I love your optimism, kiddo, but I highly doubt that was the last death trap."

We paused long enough to drink some water and examine the map again. Nash tapped the rudimentary drawing of a cave. "We must be getting close to the vault entrance by now. I'd put money on more booby traps being inside." Olav's map didn't go beyond the cave entrance, so we had no way of knowing how deep inside the mountain we'd have to go.

"True. But they'll be built on childhood games. How bad could they be?"

"With our luck, pretty damn bad." Nash eyed my backpack. "You brought the alpine draws with the rest of the climbing gear, right?"

I patted my backpack. "Yup. I brought everything we'll need." Probably. Since I'd packed gear for both of us, I'd opted for bare necessities over lugging along gadgets for every occasion.

"Let's get this over with." Nash said with none of the enthusiasm I was feeling. He tucked his empty water bottle in his own backpack and then picked up the pace.

Vegetation grew sparser at this altitude, soon giving way

to a rocky cliff that rose above us. Before long, we hit a dead-end where the trail ended abruptly, with nowhere to go but straight up. While I dug out our ropes and harnesses, Nash shielded his eyes from the late afternoon sun as he planned our ascent.

He swore. "Might as well put those away."

I followed his gaze until I spotted the cave entrance at the top of what had to be at least a fifty-foot highball without crevices for anchors. The opening looked wide enough to shimmy through. Hopefully, the cave itself would be tall enough to stand up in. Otherwise, Nash would be putting that army crawl practice to good use while I shifted into my smaller and more sure-footed goat.

The biggest challenge would be making it to the cave without safety gear. Fortunately, there was a clear way up. Beyond the giant stair-step symbol etched into the side of the mountain, footholds had been carved from the rock itself. Even with the slight rock ledges, it would be a difficult climb.

"You see that symbol?" I asked. "That's the symbol for the climbing wall my dad built for us."

Nash squinted at me. "Your dad built a fifty-foot climbing wall in your backyard?"

"Nah. It was only half that high."

"But the pattern of footholds was the same?" he asked.

I bit my lip. "Pretty much."

Nash paled as he stared up at it. "Great."

I squeezed his shoulder. "You worry too much. As a child, I climbed that wall so many times I could do it blindfolded." I pointed at the first row of footholds. "All I need to do is stick to the route he taught me." When none of the tension left Nash's rigid body, I nudged him with my hip. "You stay here and keep watch. I've got this."

"Absolutely not. You lead. I'll follow." He grabbed my back-pack and started piling anything he deemed non-essential on the ground to lighten my load.

I put my hands on my hips and raised a brow. "Nash, have you ever climbed without a safety harness?"

"Sure."

It sounded like a lie, but the stubborn set of his jaw told me he'd be following whether I liked it or not. I flicked the shark-tooth necklace he wore that hid the chip of Alatyr stone. "This talisman might save you from dying when you plummet down that drop, but healing twenty broken bones is gonna suck."

Nash threaded my arms through the straps of my back-pack like I was kid embarking on my first day of kinder-garten. After snugging the straps, he patted my head. "Special forces, remember? Worry about yourself, kiddo."

I sighed. That Green Beret bullshit was getting old. "Pay attention to where I put my feet, old man. I shift into a goat, not a mule to cart you down this mountain."

Nash laughed and prodded me to get moving.

CHAPTER 14

*D*espite the footholds, the recent precipitation made the rock slick and the holds tricky. I resisted the urge to constantly check Nash's progress as I climbed with exaggerated slowness to ensure he could follow.

"Doing okay down there?" I called when we hit the halfway point.

"As okay as a man can be while clinging to the side of a rock like a slug."

"Almost there," I assured him, concentrating on precise hand and foot placements.

When we neared the top, Nash's yell froze my momentum. I craned my neck to peer down at him. A small hawk swooped overhead before dive-bombing him. Because swatting at it was out of the question, he did his best to make himself a smaller target, tucking chin to chest and pressing closer to the mountain.

"All clear," he said when the bird finally gave up. "Let's finish this."

I relaxed and reached above me to grasp the next foothold. Before I could pull myself up, the sound of crumbling rock sent my heart racing. Below me, Nash maintained a precarious hold with his right hand while his other hand clutched nothing but rubble. The hawk must've distracted him enough that he didn't see which one I'd gripped.

Rather than pull myself higher, I dropped down far enough I could extend a leg close to Nash. "Use me as your anchor."

He made no move to reach for me, shaking his head. "I'm too heavy."

"You'll be a lot heavier busted up at the bottom of this mountain," I argued as I adjusted my balance and tightened my grip. "Besides, I'm stronger than I look. Shifter, remember? Grab on before the hawk comes back, or worse—those vamps catch up to us."

For a second, I worried his stubbornness would win out. But after a brief hesitation, his hand wrapped around my calf. Nash found his footing right as my own hand slipped.

"Damn it, Riley. I told you I was too heavy."

I gritted my teeth. It took a couple tries, but I finally regained my hold.

The rest of the climb went more smoothly, and soon enough, I was on solid ground. Once I'd pulled myself into the cave, I flipped my body around and extended both arms to Nash.

He glared up at me. "You solid this time?"

"Yes. Now, come on."

Nash gripped my forearm with one hand while clinging to the top foothold with the other. It was awkward, but he powered himself the rest of the way up. Fortunately, the space inside the cave was far taller than the opening, allowing us to stand and move around comfortably. Although the sun was setting, enough light filtered through the opening that I could see our supplies. After Nash and I ate a handful of trail mix for energy, I tossed him one of the headlamps I brought.

He dropped it like it was on fire. "Absolutely not."

I fitted mine over my forehead and flipped on the light, shining it down on the matching unicorn head lamp next to his thigh. "No one is going to see you."

He begrudgingly put it on, the little pink horn lighting up along with the glowing eyes when he turned it on. When I reached for the phone, he looked murderous. "Don't even think about taking a picture for the group chat."

If I hadn't left my cell at our vacation rental, I'd be snapping a photo for sure. But since I didn't have it, I was stuck with our sat phone. "Relax. I'm checking in with Dez before he freaks out because he can't get ahold of us in here." I scooted toward the opening, dialed Dez's number, and leaned my head outside while the phone rang.

I gave Dez a quick-and-dirty update. He told me the group that landed on the island earlier had made their way inland, but he lost sight of them in the tree cover. I warned him why we'd be unreachable so he wouldn't worry and then hung up.

As we made our way deeper into the cave, we split our attention, with Nash watching the wall on the right for symbols and me monitoring the left side of the cave. Our route narrowed to a corridor that forced us to continue single file.

A few feet in, I braced my arm across the opening to halt Nash's progress. "Hold up." I shined my beam at the symbol etched midway up the cave wall.

Nash groaned. "Tell me that's not a volcano."

"Nailed it," I sing-songed. "You ever play the floor is lava when you were a kid?" Taking his swearing as a no, I explained the only rule. "Don't touch the ground."

He surveyed the area in front of us. "Looks like dirt to me." He dug a granola bar out of his pack and tossed it down the corridor. The second it landed, the ground bubbled up red hot and turned our snack to ash.

I poked him in the ribs. "Dude. You could've at least tossed the freeze-dried beans. I liked those granola bars."

"At least now we have a preview of how fast we'll burn if we slip." He rubbed the back of his neck. "We should've kept the climbing equipment."

"Bah. We don't need fancy gear." I flipped my backpack around, so I could carry it on my front. Then, I braced my back against one wall and walked my feet up the other side. "We'll scootch our way across."

It took us twenty minutes and a couple close calls, but we made it.

Nash wiped his sweaty palms on his shirt and stared at me. "How many games did you play as a kid?"

"Quite a few." I kept walking. "Hopefully, there's no underground shark-infested waters."

"I'm too old for this shit."

"You can always tap out, old man, and wait here."

Nash grunted. "Keep moving, Cruz."

A few minutes later, Nash's light overlapped mine to illuminate a carved circle. "Let me guess, Ring Around the Rosie?"

"Pfft. Please." I rubbed my hands together. "Dodgeball."

"Wonderful," Nash muttered. "I'm sure that won't hurt at all when we're pummeled with twenty-pound rocks." He aimed his head lamp at the heavy rocks cradled in giant sling-shots aimed at us.

"It'll only hurt if you get hit." I moved in front of him and reached behind me. "Give me your hands." When he complied, I placed them on my hips. "The first few times I played dodge-ball, I got hammered."

He pinched my side. "Not helping."

"But my dad was predictable. He always threw the balls to the same places, almost like it was choreographed." Now that I knew he'd used our games to train me for this gauntlet, the predictability made sense. Back then though, I'd been down-right smug about outsmarting him. I dredged up an image of my dad's proud smile the first time I made it through a game unscathed. Then, I bent my knees and rolled my neck to repeat that performance. "Stick close to me, and those rocks will never touch you."

"We should go over the route," Nash suggested.

"On three." When I hit one, I ran for the other side, trusting him to keep up.

Rocks littered the ground by the time we reached safety, but not one clipped us. Beyond the dodgeball field was what we came for.

Nash breathed a sigh of relief at the sight of the vault door. "Please tell me you can crack it."

"I haven't encountered a vault yet that I couldn't." As I examined it, I saw it was far from a typical door. There was no key code, no biometric lock. The door itself was constructed of heavy steel with a series of handprints etched into the surface, including a bump-out with handprints on either side.

Nash spotted the symbol above the vault before I did. "Is that a baby rattle?"

This clue was the hardest to decipher. When the memory finally came, I grinned. "That's freaking brilliant. No one would guess ever this one."

Nash narrowed his eyes. "What's the game?"

I cracked my knuckles and winked. "Watch and learn." Then, I clapped my way through Down Down Baby.

And just like that, we were in.

CHAPTER 15

hen we cracked open the door, I'd expected to find a treasure trove of stolen goods. After all, my mother had a secret life stealing priceless artifacts. What I found inside the vault was even more precious.

Next to the chalice the Enclave sent me to retrieve was a collection of rare blood-fire tourmaline crystals nestled in a velvet-lined box. Because we'd once sourced one identical to these to fool Zara Bellarose, I knew the five crystals laid out here would've cost my parents a fortune. Beneath the crystals, I found instructions about how to retrieve the memories from them along with a note penned in my mother's loopy handwriting.

Darling Girl,

If you stopped in the village before finding this vault, you've probably discovered that your father and I adopted you as a toddler with your grandfather's blessing. I need you to know we loved you from the moment we gazed into those wide blue eyes of yours. You taught us how to love with our whole hearts, and we were better for it.

Guard these crystals zealously, for they hold the memories of who we are and why you came to live with us. Over the years, we've added other memories to this collection to help prepare you for whatever is coming. We wanted to spare you the fight, but if you're reading this, we failed on that front. Our deepest hope is that we gave you a life filled with happy memories as well as the strength and skills to face your future.

In this life and the next, all our love,

Mom & Dad

A single tear dripped onto the page, the ink smearing when I wiped it away. I cried harder at its loss. One less word I had to remember them by.

Nash uncurled my fingers and eased the letter from my hands. He placed it in the envelope addressed to me. Then, he folded me in his arms and held me as I wept.

When I was all cried out, I wiped my cheeks and loaded the contents of the vault into my backpack. Careful to lock the box holding the crystals, I cushioned it in the center of my supplies. I tossed the chalice to Nash to add to the stockpile of weapons in his pack.

By the time we made it out of the cave, dusk had fallen. Because there were still vamps searching the island, we turned off our headlamps, relying on the moon to light our way. We didn't make it far before the sat phone rang.

"Hey Dez," I answered. "We have the artifact."

"That's great," he said. "But we've got a problem."

I stopped walking and tapped Nash's shoulder to get his attention. "What kind of problem?" I exchanged a worried look with Nash.

"The party that landed on the beach hours ago weren't vamps." Dez paused like he didn't want to drop the next bit of news. "It's Zara Bellarose and some hired guns."

I kicked a rock. "I thought you had eyes on her." There was no way she could make it here in the time since Dez identified her on security footage.

"So did I. Something was nagging at me though, so I rewatched the video over and over until I realized what it was. On the security footage, she looked exactly like Bellarose, but the woman who walked through the front door had to be at least five foot ten."

"Shit." I dropped my head to my chest. "It was an illusion. She must've known we'd hack into the security cameras around her penthouse, and she cast an illusion spell on one of her lackeys to make us think she was there." Even though the woman on the footage wasn't her, it didn't necessarily mean Bellarose was here on the island. "How can you be sure she's here?" I asked Dez. "You said the entire party wore head-to-toe black tactical gear."

"They did. But as soon as I knew that she wasn't at her penthouse, I checked her financial trail. There are several charges in Norway." Dez sighed. "I've arranged for a pickup, but no one was willing to brave the water around the island at night. The earliest I can get someone there is in the morning. Keep your heads down until then."

I blew out a breath. "Will do. Thanks for the warning."

After I hung up, I filled Nash in on the details he hadn't already guessed from hearing my side of that conversation.

"No one will find us if we don't want to be found," Nash promised.

Thanks to his background, I was confident he'd be able to camouflage our presence. But I had no intention of hunkering down out here until morning. I slid off my backpack and thrust it toward him.

He made no move to take it from me. "What are you doing?"

I laid it on the ground by his feet. "You keep these crystals safe for me and that artifact out of Bellarose's hands." I sat on the ground and took off my shoes and jacket. "We've got ten hours—give or take—stuck on this island. I'm going to make the most of it."

"Even if Bellarose isn't at the village, she'll have her guys watching it," he warned. "You can't go back there, Riley. Not now."

I shimmied out of my jeans and added them to the pile. "Now might be all I get, Nash." I thought about Maria Baca, and my assumption that there'd always be time for another visit at a more convenient time and the realization that life rarely worked like that. "As a goat, no one will give me a second glance. Not on this island."

Nash scowled. "I don't like it." He dug out my dagger and offered it to me. "At least take this with you."

"I'm positive showing up as a goat with a demon blade strapped to my side is going to draw attention." I made a spinning motion with my finger to warn him my shirt was coming off next.

With a curse, Nash turned around and put the dagger away. When I was on four legs, he grabbed my horns and stared into my eyes. "Be careful."

When he let go, I bleated and head butted him playfully in the leg. It was the closest I could get to an agreement in this form. At his nod, I raced down the mountain, not willing to waste a single minute that could be spent getting to know my grandfather.

As I ran, I thought of all the questions I wanted to ask Olav. He could tell me stories about my birth father that I could tuck away alongside my memories of Amelia and Santiago. What had Henrik been like as a child? Had he played the same games as I had? Read the same books?

Olav could tell me about our people and share a bit of our history. I had so many questions. Was the herd on this island the only one, or were there more out there like us? I wondered if the Enclave knew about our resistance to magic, or if that ability was a closely guarded secret to prevent supernaturals from fearing us, or worse yet, using us.

I was so preoccupied with the things I wanted to ask him that it took me until I was almost there before I registered the cloying scent of smoke drifting my way. The village came into view with fire blasting right past the wards. I skidded to a stop and surveyed the carnage. The fire consumed those quaint wooden cottages far too quickly for it to be natural.

Some of the younger shifters who'd led us to the village earlier were now helping the elders escape the flames. I searched desperately for Olav's white hair and weathered face, but I didn't see him among them. Right as I was about to join the fray, I saw Jakob's broad shoulders part the crowd, a coughing Olav cradled against his chest as he carried him beyond the wards to higher ground.

Reassured that Olav was taken care of, I turned my attention to the woman at the center of it all. She stood like an avenging god, her wild blonde hair whipping around her shoulders. Zara Bellarose raised her arms, directing her elemental magic as it fanned the flames. I sprinted toward her, lowering my horns to batter her legs and gouge her unprotected stomach. She hit the ground and scooted away to put distance between us.

My shift was the fastest I'd ever managed. I didn't care that

I was naked, only that I had a voice. "Why would you do this?" I yelled.

Bellarose got to her feet and faced me, her guards still too far away to shield her.

I swept my arms wide, shaking from rage as I took in the destruction she'd caused. "All this to get your hands on a demon artifact. These people didn't even have it." Smoke wrapped around my throat and burned into my lungs, but my voice was steady. "You're never going to get your hands on that chalice," I vowed.

Bellarose laughed as she put more distance between us. "Keep your little trinket."

I kept her in my sights despite my eyes burning from the smoke and ash floating in the air around us. "If you're not here for the vessel, then why did you come?"

"Oh child, you haven't realized it, yet? You are the vessel. And this," she smiled as the village burned, "this is because Olav Larsen hid you from me." With a jerk of her head, the men she'd brought with her surrounded us. She snapped her fingers. "Bring her."

It might be four against one, but I wasn't going to make this easy. Too bad I hadn't listened to Nash and strapped that dagger to my side. It'd come in handy right about now. All three of Bellarose's hired guns wore black baseball hats pulled low over their eyes and balaclavas to mask their features. They were big, anonymous, and menacing.

They sized me up—a lone woman standing before them naked and unarmed—and dismissed me as an easy target, choosing to come at me one at a time rather than en masse. As the first one lunged, I bent to the earth, gathered a fistful of dirt, and tossed it into his eyes before sweeping his leg. Seeing their buddy go down, the other two flanked me. Although I managed an elbow to the nose of one man and a throat punch to the other, they had me on the ground with a knee in my back within minutes.

When the man I'd tossed dirt at went for the zip ties, it was clear I wouldn't win this fight with brute force or grappling maneuvers. So, I reached for the only weapon I had. I'd borrowed a witch's magic once. If ever there was a time to do it again, this was it. Before they could secure my wrists, I lifted a hand in Bellarose's direction. Then, I closed my eyes and concentrated on her power.

Her strangled gasp told me she must've felt the tug. I opened myself to the magic, feeling the elemental power flowing into me like a sledgehammer.

"Stop!" Bellarose yelled.

I assumed the order was for me. But the knee in my back eased and the hands pinning me to the ground let go. As I scrambled to my feet before the men could change their minds, my hold on her magic slipped.

Bellarose rubbed the center of her chest while she stared at me with a pride that soured my stomach. "You're ready, then." She turned and walked away, her bodyguards closing ranks around her as they headed for the beach. "I'll be seeing you soon, daughter. After all, we have a prophecy to fulfill."

All the fears I hadn't allowed myself to linger on crashed down on me. No matter who she was to me, I needed to chase her down, put an end to her evil. Before I could act on that urge, big hands grabbed me by the shoulders. I blinked up at Jakob's pale face.

"Let her go," Jakob said. "Right now, you need to come with me to say your goodbyes. Olav won't make it through the night." He pulled his shirt over his head and handed it to me, waiting until I was covered to lead the way.

I stumbled after him, numbness making it feel like I was in someone else's body. All the way there, I prayed for Jakob to be wrong. The second I saw the coughs wracking Olav's frail body, I knew he was right. I dropped to my knees, the hard-packed earth slamming into my shins.

"Don't cry, sweetheart." Olav wiped tears from my cheek and clutched my hand between his. "It's okay. Now that I've seen you again, I can die a happy man."

The tears came so fast, they threatened to drown me. I couldn't speak.

Olav squeezed my hands. "After Henrik died, I was too lost to my own grief to be a good grandfather to you. If I could go back to those days, I would treasure the time with you." A cough rattled his chest. "I missed so much. Tell me about your childhood. Were you happy?"

I looked into those eyes that mirrored my own and saw the hope shining in them. While smoke blanketed the village and grief made my chest ache, I told my grandfather what he needed to hear.

"I was so happy, Olav. Amelia and Santiago were the best parents I could've asked for. There was never a day when I didn't feel their love." I smiled, battling back the tears, as I told him about my life with them, leaving out the years with Carl's pack that came after. And when he confessed he was worried I'd be all alone in the world, I told him all about my witches, my friends, and my mate.

In the early hours before dawn, my grandfather died holding my hand, at peace with the decision he'd made twenty-two years ago.

CHAPTER 16

*G*rief wasn't proportionate to the depth of a relationship. Often, we grieved harder for the ones stolen from us than those we spent a lifetime with. A day ago, I didn't know Olav existed. And yet, I curled into the plush seat of the jet carrying me home, and I mourned the lost years and the future moments we'd never have.

Other than strong-arming me into eating and drinking, Nash and Dez let me be. The twelve-hour flight allowed me to replay every brief interaction I had with Olav. It also gave me time to come to terms with what I needed to do about this demon prophecy. Coping with the knowledge that the witch responsible for blowing up my apartment and orchestrating Martha Matthews' and Owen Hughes' attacks turned out to be my mother would take a hell of a lot longer.

Seven hours into our flight, I tamped down my sorrow and got to work. Forty thousand feet in the air limited our resources, but online Wi-Fi gave us the opportunity to continue cyberstalking Zara Bellarose. Thanks to Dez, I had her last month's bank transactions, her medical history, and the location of the strip mall where she got her nails done. What I didn't know was whether she was working with the demons or at odds with them. Despite fast-forwarding through days of street cam and security footage, the only people we witnessed coming or going from her penthouse were Bellarose herself, a contingent of armed guards, and her mystery guest who never left the building without a hooded cloak.

Frustrated but too wound up to nap, I abandoned Dez's laptop and started texting. First, I let Sato know that I'd secured his precious artifact. Then, I messaged the group chat with a bare bones update of what happened. Some things I didn't want to commit to text, so I kept Bellarose's words and my cargo of crystals to myself for now.

By the time we landed in Kansas City, both Volkov and Sato awaited us at the airport. I left Nash to hand over the demon artifact while I crashed into Volkov's solid body. His arms closed around me, his familiar scent of cedarwood and spice calming the emotional tempest that threatened to pull me under.

When I let go of Volkov to deal with the Enclave's mouthpiece, Kage Sato was watching me like a zoo exhibit. "Why are you so upset?" he asked, those dark eyes assessing.

"I don't know. I suppose watching a village burn to the ground does that to a person." I hadn't told Sato who lived in the village, only that Bellarose showed up with armed guards to torch the island. I let him believe she was chasing the chalice he now held. And I certainly didn't share the revelations she'd hurled at me on the beach.

He studied the artifact in his hands. "And she didn't try to take this from you?" Sato studied me. "That seems odd, doesn't it?"

I shrugged. "I didn't give her the chance."

When Sato kept staring at me, a warning growl rumbled through Volkov's chest. "You got what you came for, assassin. We're leaving."

"I have questions for Riley first," Sato insisted.

"Not tonight, you don't." Volkov didn't wait around for Sato's response, ushering me across the lot and into the passenger seat of his Audi. Seeing the way my fingers trembled, he reached down and turned on the heated seat before buckling me in and closing my door.

On the way to headquarters, I told him everything. Even the bits I wished I didn't know.

Volkov listened to all of it without judgment as he navigated in and out of traffic like a Nascar driver. "Do you want to be alone tonight?" From the iron grip Volkov had on the steering wheel when he asked, he hated the idea of leaving me on my own. But he'd do it if that's what I needed.

After all the shocks of the past few days, the last thing I wanted was to be alone with my thoughts though. I craved the comfort of familiar surroundings and proximity to the people I loved. "Definitely not."

Volkov relaxed. "Good because Helen called earlier to say she was rallying the troops, and they'd meet us at headquarters. I would've ditched her if you asked, but," he grimaced, "I'd rather not risk that witch's wrath."

I laughed, probably as he'd intended.

When we arrived at headquarters, Helen and the girls were already fluffing the boatload of pillows they'd brought over and arranging a week's worth of snacks on my bar top. Nash and Dez came in on our heels. As soon as he heard Nash's voice, Garth raced out from behind my oversized couch to greet his roomie.

Nash stared at the vengeance demon. "What is he wearing?"

"Pajamas," Helen said cheerfully, coming to join us. "Alyce made them. Aren't they adorable?"

Garth inflated his chest and preened, showing off the chicken-sized pajama pants covered in flames. The rhinestone Demon across his fluffy butt must be Bea's doing. Because he wasn't exactly shaped for pants, Alyce included suspenders to keep them on. Bea's new cat, Circe, wound around the rooster, brushing up against his feathers, much to his annoyance. When Garth crowed in her face, Circe offered him her backside, swishing her tail and slapping it against his beak.

Nash grimaced as he watched them. "But why is he wearing pajamas?"

Helen flicked Nash's ear. "Because it's a party, that's why. Now tell my boy how handsome he looks."

Garth waited expectantly for Nash to mutter his compliment before sauntering away, ignoring his new cat shadow. Bea handed Nash a matching pair of pajama pants with Human spelled out in rhinestones. Nash dropped them like they were made of actual flames.

When I chuckled at their antics, Volkov pressed a kiss to the top of my head. Coming home to the chaos of my friends and family soothed me in a way few things could.

Helen tossed Dez a pair of pajama pants next.

He caught and inspected smiled. They were a computer nerd's ideal wardrobe staple with tiny ones and zeros all over the print. "Hey, I have these exact pants at home," Dez said.

Alyce giggled from behind the bar where she was unpacking mystery Jello surprises. "That's because those are yours, silly."

"Very funny." Dez narrowed his eyes at the girls. "My security system is state-of-the-art. No way you got past it."

"Sure did." Helen smiled sweetly and patted his arm. "We asked Arlo to help us."

The rest of us flinched.

Dez's face turned so red it matched his hair as he sputtered in outrage. "How could you let the enemy into my apartment?"

"Actually, Arlo let us in." Helen ignored his outraged gasp and turned to us. One look at Max Volkov in all his three-piece-suit glory, and she huffed. "Why are you dressed like that?"

Volkov glanced at his impeccable charcoal gray suit, then at her. "I always dress like this."

Bea sidled up to me and nudged me in the ribs. "Even in the bedroom?" She wiggled her penciled-in blonde brows. "Kinky."

"How on earth is that kinky?" Dez asked.

I clasped my hand over Bea's mouth before she could regale us with tales of her fling with a suit-wearing copy machine salesman. Her eyes twinkled, but she kept her stories to herself when I let her go.

Helen thumped Volkov's tie. "What kind of stick-in-the-mud wears a suit to a pajama party?"

He frowned. "I assumed you were joking about that part."

Alyce looked scandalized. "We would never joke about pajama night."

The other three witches nodded solemnly.

Bea waved a stuffed tote bag in the air. "Don't you worry, sugar. I came prepared."

Volkov straightened his tie and glared at her. "Not happening, witch."

Ten minutes later, he was decked out in cat pajama pants that were at least a size too small.

Bea wolf whistled. "Looking mighty fine there, alpha."

Janis and Bea snickered. Volkov glared at them both, which made them laugh harder.

The last to join us, Kali and Craig stopped in the open doorway to gape at Volkov. "What in the name of decency are you even wearing?" Kali whispered. "Are those dancing kittens?"

Craig's broad shoulders shook with laughter as he took in his boss's new duds.

Bea winked up at Craig. "Glad you approve, big guy, because I've got a little something for you, too." She slapped a pair of gray lounge pants into his arms. They looked normal until he flipped them over where the words Rock Hard were scrawled across the bum in pink puff paint. Craig held them away from his body like they were radioactive.

Volkov crossed his arms over his bare chest and smiled. "Best get changed, Ward."

Recognizing a losing battle when he wandered into one, Craig let Kali steer him into the bathroom. When they returned, Craig had on the snug gray pants and was shirtless, thanks to Bea's insistence.

Bea hummed in approval.

Not trusting Bea's fashion sense after the whole apron fiasco over Christmas, Kali had brought along her own PJs. In true Kali style, they were retro silk hemmed with black lace. She even wore fuzzy glam slippers.

When I disappeared downstairs and returned wearing plaid flannel pants and a plain black tank top, no one objected. Between that and the sympathy radiating off my witches, it was obvious the guys had filled them in on my trip while I changed.

Helen shoved a bowl of popcorn into my arms and marched me over to the couch, burying me in pillows.

"Now then. Do you need to have a good cry or an excuse to scream? Because we can do monster movies or a chick flick marathon." Helen shushed the collective groan that went up from the men and handed me the remote. "Your call, hon."

CHAPTER 17

$\mathcal{I}$t took me two days to be ready to open the walnut box that held my parents' memories. Although I'd steeled myself for whatever information I was about to discover, at least I didn't have to face it alone. Like they had every day since I'd landed in Kansas City as a runaway sixteen-year-old, Helen and the girls gave me their support. Volkov asked Teagan to handle pack business today so that he could be here with me as well.

After gathering the supplies we needed, we all met at headquarters. Dez and Nash were already sprawled out on the couch, game controllers in hand. I bypassed the guys to greet the rooster marching back and forth across the coffee table like he was directing the action playing out on the screen. "Hey Garth." He paused long enough for me to stroke his feathers and coo about what a fierce boy he was before resuming his pacing.

Helen glared at Nash and Dez with her hands on her hips. "If I'd known you two were wasting time playing video games,

I would've taken my Garth to Magic Paws where he gets enrichment activities and socialization."

Nash muttered about demon bonding under his breath, earning a thwack on the back of the head from Helen. He scooted forward and kept playing.

"Hey! This qualifies as an enrichment activity. It's like army simulations," Dez argued as he took out another player.

Garth crowed his agreement, his eyes glowing like embers at the on-screen carnage.

When Nash mocked the idea of video games qualifying as simulations, Dez merely smiled and pointed to the screen with his controller. "As you can see from the score, Nash here needs all the practice he can get." Video games were the one place where Dez was a better shot than Nash, and he wasn't above gloating about it.

At Volkov's chuckle, Nash held out his controller. "You think you can do better? You're welcome to try."

Dez grinned and scooted over.

Volkov straightened his tie, making no move to take Nash up on his offer. "I don't play war games." His eyes blazed amber. "But any time you two want to go toe-to-toe in the field, I'll be more than happy to demonstrate my abilities."

Bea glanced between Volkov and Nash. "Oh sugar, tell me there's gonna be baby oil and an inflatable pool involved in this challenge." She licked her fuchsia lips and winked at them.

All three men stared at her. She grinned, unrepentant, as Volkov took off his jacket, rolled up his sleeves, and joined me in the space we'd cleared to perform the memory retrieval spell.

Nash and Dez returned their attention to their game, grumbling when Helen marched in front of the television to get to our little magical library. Thanks to Bea's regular contributions, the bookshelves now overflowed with magical tomes, including the grimoire with the memory retrieval spell.

Helen opened the well-worn grimoire to a bookmarked page. "You sure you're ready, hon?"

I nodded. "Yeah. I need to do this."

If she'd let me, I'd binge through these memories one after the other. But since Helen insisted that would be far too dangerous, I had to settle for one a day. Each blood-fire tourmaline crystal was nestled inside the velvet-lined box and labeled with a name. My hand shook as I lifted the first of Santiago's memories from the box Volkov held open for me.

Nerves made my t-shirt feel too tight. I stretched the neckline, took a deep breath, and gestured for Helen to begin. As she recited the incantation, I sliced my palm and pressed it to the surface. The tourmaline crystal glowed like hellfire from my offering. Blood magic thickened the air, causing goosebumps to break out along my arms and Garth's head to swivel our direction, his eyes as bright as the crystal. I didn't like the feel of this magic, but it was the only way.

There was no easing into the memory. One second, I clutched a cold crystal in my blood-slicked palm. The next, I stood in an unfamiliar alley with my back to the wall.

I wasn't a passive observer watching someone else's memory.

I became my father.

The damp stone wall at my back and the man stalking toward me should've sent fear skittering across my skin. This was the sort of dark alley serial killers scoped out for their next victim. And yet, all I felt was irritation as I waited for him.

I caught sight of my reflection in a nearby window—a

young man with hard eyes and a no-nonsense buzz cut, the distinct bulge of a gun hidden beneath my jacket.

"Why are you here?" I demanded.

The man stopped in front me and glanced around to ensure no one was listening before answering. "I have an assignment for you, Shadow."

I pushed off the wall and took a step toward the man who now held his hands up as if to ward off the devil. Typical pencil pusher. He might have masked up and tossed on a trench coat for this meetup like he was playing spy, but I recognized that nasally voice. Steve was one of the Enclave's favorite boot lickers. He always had his sharp nose in everyone else's missions.

I gave myself a second to enjoy the way he squirmed uncomfortably while I sized him up. "I already have a job, as you well know, Steve." I wasn't thrilled about being ordered to play babysitter to a human thief, even if it was to go after a rare artifact rumored to be the linchpin to a demon prophecy. But my job was to carry out whatever mission the Enclave handed me, not to question it.

Steve's eyes widened at my casual use of his name before he hastily adjusted his mask. "You have the on-the-books job. This one is off the books." Steve's brown eyes flared with the kind of fanaticism that bred atrocities as he said it.

In the ten years I'd been a Shadow, I'd become numb to the death I delivered, but I'd never reveled in it. Not like Steve. Maybe that was because men like Steve were never the ones with blood-stained hands.

Whatever assignment he had, I wasn't going to like it.

I checked my watch. "Get to your point. I've got shit to do."

"This job is for Cerberus."

My hand was around his throat before he registered the

movement. "Whatever you're playing at, Steve. I'm not interested."

Cerberus was the code name for the black ops I'd been carrying out for the past two years. Unlike normal Enclave jobs like covert surveillance and sanctioned assassinations handed down through official channels, Cerberus assignments came through an encrypted app. Although most Shadows had heard the whispered rumors about our black ops unit, the anonymity of how we worked ensured operatives didn't have enough incriminating information to tank more than their current assignment should they be caught.

I didn't even know how many of us there were. The only other operative I'd met in person had been the Shadow who'd recruited—and trained—me. And that wasn't pencil-pushing Steve here. I tightened my grip until Steve's hands clutched at my arm and his eyes bulged.

"Check the app," he croaked when I let up the pressure enough for him to suck in a breath.

I shoved him away from me. Only operatives knew about the encrypted app, so he was either one of us or laying a trap. "What app would that be?"

He glared at me as he rubbed his throat. "Cute." Then, he nodded toward the pocket of my jacket where I kept my cell phone.

As soon as I pulled it out, I saw the notification. The message consisted of today's date, this location, and the current time. Apparently, Steve was team Cerberus. I wondered if he'd taken it upon himself to break protocol and meet me in person.

"What's the assignment?"

Steve stepped closer, his eyes animated despite his scratchy voice. "You're going to bring in the vessel."

I frowned. That was precisely the next job the Enclave had already assigned me—to escort the human thief to an uninhabited island off the coast of Norway to secure Zagan's chalice.

At my furrowed brow, Steve smiled and passed me a burlap bag. I peered inside to see a chalice matching the description of our artifact. "What's this?"

"The decoy." Steve's gaze swept through the dark alley again. "It's what you'll hand over to the Enclave."

Unease coiled in my gut. In the years I'd been running ops for Cerberus, my assumption had always been that these missions were carried out at the direction of the full Enclave. I'd figured the secrecy was due to the nature of the tasks. But if I was supposed to turn over a decoy, it meant Cerberus was but one faction within a fractured Enclave.

As years of brutal training at the Compound taught me though, I left the ethics to those pulling the strings and asked the only question that mattered for a man like me. "What's the real target?"

"Not what," Steve corrected. "Who."

I came out of the memory as fast as I'd fallen into it, gulping in heavy breaths. Helen's fast reflexes saved the crystal when I fumbled it. She nestled it in its box and handed me a glass of water and a vanilla wafer. I nibbled the cookie while I got my bearings, then I told everyone what I saw in that memory.

A vein pulsed in Volkov's forehead. "Your father was a Shadow."

I nodded. "Yeah. He was."

"Do you think Sato knew?" Dez asked.

"Maybe." I replayed all my conversations with Kage Sato that involved my parents. Nothing stood out as a tell, but then again, the man had a world-class poker face. "I'm not sure why he'd keep that information to himself if he did know." He'd told me my mom was a thief. Why keep this from me? "Even if he knew my dad was the Shadow sent to guard my mom while she stole the artifact, he must not know I'm the vessel. Otherwise, there'd be no reason to send me after the chalice now. But that doesn't mean Sato isn't part of this Cerberus project, whatever that is." From my dad's memory, the anonymity Cerberus maintained made it entirely possible Sato and my dad were both part of the same black ops group without knowing the other's identity.

I turned to Volkov. "What do you know about this Cerberus project?"

A muscle working in Volkov's jaw. "Not enough. There were rumors of a black ops unit, but most of us chalked it up to myth."

That tracked with Santiago's memory.

"I'll reach out to Aleksei," Volkov offered.

As the head of the compound, Volkov's brother Aleksei would know more than most about a secret unit operating within the Shadows. Whether he'd share any of that knowledge with his brother was another matter since the two had been estranged for years. And yet, Volkov was willing to reach out for me.

I wrapped my arms around his waist for a quick hug. "Thank you."

Nash set aside his controller. "Sounds like at least part of the Enclave has their own agenda."

Helen closed the grimoire with a thump and slid it onto the bookshelf. "If the Enclave is at odds, we can't afford to trust any of them."

"Agreed." Volkov stiffened. "We keep this to ourselves."

Alyce twisted her skirt in her hands as she looked at me. "If the wrong person finds out you're the vessel—" she trailed off.

I finished the thought. "I'm dead." The words of the demon prophecy echoed inside my head.

Sacrifice the child who wields water and air,

destroy the vessel, weaken the forge.

"Not going to happen," Volkov swore.

Helen nodded and braced her hands on her hips. "Damn right it's not because we're going to make Riley such a threat, no one will dare come after her."

Alyce patted my shoulder, while Bea rolled up her zebra-print sleeves. "We'll start training tomorrow," Bea announced. "You need to be able to turn their own power against them."

They were right. I'd spent a lifetime powerless. It was high time I learned how to channel some magic for myself. "Let's do it."

Helen's cell phone rang, interrupting our planning. She walked into the bar area to take the call. When she ended it, her dark eyes were serious.

"What's wrong?" Given the avalanche of bad news lately, I braced myself for yet another catastrophe.

Helen pushed her shoulders back and surveyed the room, pausing to glower at Nash. "There was an incident at Magic Paws yesterday."

The fact that Garth was currently preening his feathers next to the couch assured me he was okay. "What kind of incident?"

Nash snorted. "Imagine that. Sending a vengeance demon to doggie daycare caused problems."

Helen's cheeks flushed, and she advanced on Nash. "You listen here, Wade Mitchell."

We all flinched at the full-name treatment and edged away from Nash. He crossed his arms and braced himself for Helen's ire.

She poked him in the chest. "My Garth wasn't the one who started it."

"What happened?" I asked.

Helen slumped. "You see, there was a humper."

"A humper?" Nash repeated.

Garth's hackles rose, and his eyes turned demon red. Dez grabbed a handful of popcorn leftover from our movie marathon last night and tossed it in his mouth, scooting closer for the story.

"Yes." Helen pursed her lips. "As you can imagine, our Garth here didn't take kindly to that Golden Doodle humping him."

Dez and I both snickered.

Helen shot us a dirty look. "It seems there was a bit of a kerfuffle. I've been called in for a meeting, along with the instigator's owner, to discuss the matter."

Garth pecked the seam of the couch, refusing to meet Helen's gaze.

Nash scoffed. "Like a parent teacher conference?"

Helen narrowed her eyes. "Perhaps if he didn't have such an absentee father, Garth wouldn't be acting out like this."

Garth sidled closer to Nash and crowed, looking down-right smug for a rooster. As soon as Helen's gaze swung to him, he deflated and pecked Nash's boot.

"He's not my kid." Nash stabbed a finger at Garth. "He's thousands of years old and a demon. If anything, he'd be the father in this scenario."

Garth perked up at the idea of being in charge of Nash.

Helen grabbed her purse and tossed Nash's truck keys to

him. "Let's go." She marched out the door without waiting to make sure he followed.

When Nash looked at us, I shrugged. "You should probably go. Trust me. You don't want to test Helen when she's in a mood like this."

With an annoyed sigh, Nash stalked after her. The rest of the girls took off a few minutes later, and Volkov got called out on a pack matter shortly thereafter. That left me and Dez alone.

I flopped onto the couch and groaned. "I'd hoped for a happy memory, not to find out my dad was a jerk and a super assassin."

Dez turned off the television, set aside the popcorn, and nudged his black-rimmed glasses up his nose. "How do you want to deal with it? Fight or cry?"

"Definitely fight." I was all cried out.

"Come on." Although he shot a wistful glance at the box of tissues on the coffee table, Dez pulled me to my feet and prodded me down the stairs to the gym. Because he was the best sort of friend, he strapped on MMA gloves when we got there and let me work out my feelings in the cage. For the next hour, I channeled all the anger and fear I'd bottled up the past few days into action.

While we sparred, I attempted to reconcile the good-natured man who'd taught me a donkey kick as my first self-defense move with the Shadow who'd readily agreed to kidnap an innocent child without so much a glimmer of remorse in his familiar dark eyes.

CHAPTER 18

*T*he second blood-fire tourmaline felt far heavier in my hand than the first one I'd held yesterday. This morning, only Helen and the girls were with me, as we prepared to tap into the second memory. I sat it back in its box and picked up a second donut, stalling.

Today, Dez had stayed home to Arlo-proof his apartment security system while Nash was spending quality time with his wayward roommate at Helen's insistence. A day after their Magic Paws meeting Helen was still livid about the week-long suspension Garth earned.

She ranted as the rest of us polished off Bea's homemade donuts in Helen's kitchen. "Can you believe that place? They railroaded my poor Garth while that Golden Doodle got off with a warning and a bacon-flavored dog biscuit." She slammed her hands down on the table. "It's not right."

No amount of reassurance would calm Helen down, so we all opted for a distraction instead. I picked up the crystal again, this one labeled with Amelia's name, and waited for Helen to join me with the grimoire.

I chewed my lower lip as I considered what secrets it might hold. "What if—" I couldn't finish the thought.

Helen patted my back, Garth's troubles forgotten for the moment. "Whatever your mom left for you, she did it out of love." Seeing my flinch at her use of mom, Helen shook my shoulders. "Zara Bellarose may have given birth to you, but that doesn't make her your mother. Amelia chose you, again and again. That's what family does."

My father's hard stare from the first memory still weighed me down. "And my dad?" I pressed the heel of my hand against my chest like it could stem the ache. "What if he chose me for the wrong reason?" What if I had only been a job to him? The possibility my dad had engineered our scavenger hunts and backyard obstacle courses, not out of love, but in preparation for whatever role Cerberus intended for me felt like a betrayal.

Helen flicked my ear. "You listen to me, young lady. The only thing that matters is that they did choose you. Don't let the Enclave's puppeteering steal your parents' love from you."

It took me a second to breathe through the tears, so I could answer. "You're right. Amelia and Santiago were my parents." Whatever his motivation had been, Santiago had been a good father to me. I pulled all the girls in for a group hug. "Just like you're my family."

Helen sniffled and then boxed my ears for making her cry. She picked up the grimoire again and motioned for me to hurry up.

"I'm ready," I said, even though I was far from it.

When we were all in position, Helen began chanting the spell to thrust me into another memory. I focused on the steady cadence of Helen's voice as I was pulled under. It took several seconds to acclimate.

This time, I was Amelia, swaying on the deck of a boat as we approached my grandfather's island. Salt-water air parched my throat, and cold wind seeped beneath my clothes. As I stared at the island mountains jutting from the sea, my heart raced, both from the anticipation of a big heist and from a dread I couldn't explain.

Something was not right.

I glanced at the man who hovered like a storm cloud next to me. Tall, broad-shouldered, and heart-stoppingly hand-some, my assigned bodyguard ruined every dirty thought I entertained every time he opened his big, stupid mouth. In the three days I'd known him, he'd insulted my shoes, questioned my intelligence, and outright laughed when I'd informed him the Enclave hired me for my expertise and that he should stay in his lane.

Admittedly, I probably should've kept that last thought to myself.

The man assigned to protect me on this job had the emotional range of a grapefruit and the sunny disposition of a porcupine. He also eyed me with trepidation whenever he glanced my way. Like I was the threat somehow. I snorted. The man was easily twice my weight with hands that rivaled baseball mitts. Plus, he was a walking arsenal, with knives and guns strapped all over his body. What threat could I possibly pose to a man like him?

He scanned my all-black cat burglar ensemble, frowning at the practical tactical boots on my feet. "Ready, niñita?"

I gnashed my teeth at his condescending little girl nick-name. Three days, and he had yet to address me by my actual name.

Nor had he given me his. Instead, he'd instructed me to call him El Santo with a straight face. Who gave themselves a handle like that? I couldn't decide if he was a washed-out professional wrestler chasing his glory days or merely insufferable like people who referred to themselves in third person.

I smirked up at him, purposely keeping my tone flippant and my nerves under wraps. "Get in, steal the artifact, and get out. Stay out of my way, meathead, and let me do my job." Two could play the insulting nickname game.

His lips twitched in what almost could've passed for a smile before his customary scowl slid into place.

Neither of us spoke as he rowed us the rest of the way to shore in a non-descript canoe. The waters surrounding the island were too choppy to drop us any closer. I left the rowing to him, while I mentally prepared for the biggest job I'd ever attempted. If I pulled this off, I'd be set for life.

The organization that had recruited me was more powerful than any clandestine government group I'd imagined. I was still acclimating to the knowledge that monsters were real. The vamp who gate-crashed my sentencing for first-degree burglary had been proof. Using some kind of weird mind control, the vampire persuaded the judge prepared to sentence me to twenty years to release me into his care instead. Then, the vamp compelled me to cooperate before marching me through a side exit. A representative from the Enclave was waiting. He gave me two options—do this job for them and walk away a rich woman after my memory of them had been wiped or serve as an appetizer for the bloodsucker who'd just saved me from a prison sentence.

Even without the death threat, I would've agreed. A million dollars was a lot of money for stealing the chalice they called the vessel.

I ignored the hand my bodyguard offered to help me out

of the canoe and rolled my shoulders. Go time. I lowered my ski mask, making sure to tuck my blonde hair beneath it, and headed for the path leading to my target.

Before I made it more than a couple steps, a strong hand banded around my arm and jerked me to a stop. "What?" I snapped.

My bodyguard scanned the beach for threats before spinning me to face him. "Change of plans."

Sweat beaded on the neck. Last-minute changes rarely ended well for me. The last time someone had pulled that card, I'd ended up in handcuffs. "Listen buddy, I was hired to go after this vessel, and that's exactly what I'm going to do." I tried to yank my arm out of his grip, but he held firm.

He raised a brow that made me want to punch him in the face. Given our height difference, that would be a hard swing to land, so instead, I threw my body weight behind my next attempt to break free.

"Are you finished?"

I growled, then kicked his shin when he had the nerve to smile at me.

When he was sure I'd stay put, he released me and held up a flat disc with markings etched into its surface. "You'll still get the vessel. But it's not going to be a simple snatch and grab." His voice sent chills down my spine as he chanted in a language I didn't recognize. The marks on the disc lit up before fading into a soft glow. "First, I'm going to need you to bring down the wards around the village with this." He offered it to me.

I examined the disk, brushing my fingertip over the strange marks covering it. "Wards? Like magical wards?"

He side-stepped the question, thrusting a map of a small

village into my hands and pointing to a spot on the far side. "Place the disc here and then get out."

"That's not the job." I tried to hand both the object and the map to him.

"It is now." He closed my palm around the disc. "I already have the vessel. Do this, and it's yours. Try anything else," His hand tightened on mine threatening to crush the delicate bones. "And you won't make it off this island."

I swallowed, staring at the wicked blade he palmed with his other hand. "Fine," I jerked free, and this time, he let me go. I memorized the route before slapping the map against his chest. "If you already have the vessel, then what are we stealing?"

"All you need to worry about is bringing down those wards. I'll handle the rest." He reached into his pack and pulled out a cloth and an amber-hued bottle with a chloroform label on it before tossing the backpack to the side of the trail. Then, he spun me around and pushed me toward the village.

Not sure whether the cloth was intended for me or for someone else, I didn't argue. Once I got into that village, I'd steal any weapon I could get my hands on before planting this disc. If I was lucky, he'd hand over the vessel like he said he would, and I'd end up a million dollars richer. If not, my best hope was to stab my bodyguard in the liver before he knocked me out and turned me into shark bait.

The island faded as my own consciousness rose to take the place of Amelia's memory.

I tucked away the heartache of seeing my father's face again. And I tried to scrub my mom's inappropriate thoughts about my dad from my brain. Gross.

Although I was relieved that my mom had believed she

was stealing an artifact until the last minute, I hated that my dad had been complicit. The man in these memories was nothing like the father who raised me, and I hated the idea he might've been more villain than savior. After all, Shadows were spies trained on subterfuge. How well had I actually known the man?

I'd need time to unpack all the emotions that dredged up, so I focused on another aspect of her memory. "Those assholes," I grumbled as I faced the girls.

They all crowded closer, ready to commiserate. I let Helen take the empty crystal from my hand and patted Bea's arm when she squeezed my shoulder.

Alyce's brows pinched. "What is it, sweetheart?"

"The Enclave offered my mom a million dollars to retrieve the vessel. That was twenty-some years ago."

Bea, Alyce, and Janis frowned, trying to understand why that upset me.

Helen balled her hands into fists and placed them on her hips though, as outraged as I was. "Those dirty weasels."

I nodded. "Exactly. I should've negotiated a higher fee before I stole anything for the Enclave."

Apparently, a hundred grand was far below market value for my services. If I survived this prophecy, my first order of business would be raising my rates. In the meantime, I needed to master my powers because sooner or later, whoever sent Amelia and Santiago after me was going to strike again.

CHAPTER 19

"According to this, you're rarer than chlamydia in a nunnery." Bea handed me a book and tapped the open page with a triumphant smile.

I stared at her. "Huh?"

"Nulls are rare," Helen explained, stacking another book on top of the first. "But a siphon like you are—that's a power verging on myth. You're special, Riley." Helen patted my head fondly. "Now get off your tush, so we can figure out how to stop the demons and the Enclave and the vamps from killing you. Because they're all going to try."

"Good pep talk," I muttered as I paged through the books on my lap, scanning the entries for anything that might be useful. Nothing.

Helen huffed. "If you want pretty words, you better go find that fancy wolf of yours. We're here to make sure you survive, hon." Helen wagged a finger in my face. "To do that, you need to be able to steal another witches' magic as easily as you pickpocket money clips off rich assholes."

Helen motioned to Janis, who dutifully lobbed a magical

grenade at my head. On instinct, I caught it. The buzz of magic dissipated at my touch.

Helen swatted my hand. "Not like that. You need to take the magic for yourself. Don't waste it." She turned to Janis. "This time, put your back into it."

Half an hour later, Helen's living room was littered with potion bombs, but I was no closer to siphoning magic.

Bea tilted her head, her giant feathered earrings fluttering with the movement. She grinned when she caught me staring at them. "Can you believe these were in the discount bin at the thrift store?"

Oh, I could believe it. The market for pink and teal dangly earrings dried up forty years ago. "They're a real find."

"Anyway," she bobbed her head. "I think we should try wards. Maybe it'll be easier for you to latch on to magical threads you can see."

The girls perked up at the idea. While they booby-trapped Helen's living room with dozens of magical tripwires and waterfall wards, I grabbed another book. This one was titled *Myths and Monsters* and had detailed illustrations. I flipped through the entries for any that bore my birth mother's face. Although I found pictures of Kali's demon Raum and Garth's demon Andras, Zara Bellarose hadn't made the cut. At least, not yet. At forty-six, she still had the time, and likely the aspirations, to land herself in a book just like this one.

I needed more intel on Bellarose now though. Not only was my power rooted in her DNA, she was also as dangerous as the snakes she was so fond of. Watching the girls weaving magic around me gave me an idea. Over the last couple months, Dez had dug deep into Bellarose's records to dredge up anything incriminating or illuminating. And while that gave us insight into her financial records and her daily routines, he hadn't found anything that helped us piece together her motivation. But maybe instead of digging directly into her online footprint, we needed to go wider and look at the periphery.

I texted Dez to ask if he had the skills to hack into the Witches' Council records and dig up anything related to Bellarose—professional associates, her political maneuverings for the brief time she sat on the council, investigations into the underground magic market she controlled. While the council made it a point to keep genealogical records and member lists offline, any organization as fond of red tape and meeting minutes as the Witches' Council was bound to have online records worth pilfering.

The cake emoji Dez sent as his answer, quickly followed by the middle finger, cheered me up. If anyone could dig up buried intel, it was my nerdy friend out to prove his hacking prowess. His imaginary competition with Arlo demanded it. I had yet to meet the mysterious hacker on Volkov's payroll, but one of these days, I was going to swing by to thank him for driving Nash's truck home, so we didn't have to go back for it.

Helen snapped her fingers in front of my face, dragging me back to my own challenge. "Show us what you can do, hon."

This time when I reached for the magic, it flowed into me like it had been mine all along. Janis and Alyce clapped for me. Bea whistled her approval loudly enough to make the rest of us flinch.

Helen jabbed me in the side. "Now do something with that magic."

Unfortunately, that proved more difficult. Despite several tries, my magical abilities were stunted at catch and release. Since neither book research nor practice taught me how to channel my power efficiently, we turned to the one avenue left to us—my parents' memories.

Helen grabbed her grimoire, even though she'd likely had the retrieval spell memorized by now. I lifted the third crystal with my father's name beneath it and sliced my palm, falling into this memory even quicker than I had the previous two.

The thief I watched storming out of the village bore little resemblance to the woman who'd crept into it. That nervous energy that had her bouncing on the balls of her feet in anticipation of a heist was long gone. In its place, rage flushed her cheeks and stiffened her spine. With her ski mask gone, her long, honey blonde hair practically glowed in the moonlight.

Mel Hunt was all fluff and fire as she stalked toward me. For the tenth time, I wondered how a woman like her landed herself in a life like this. She belonged tucked safely into a pretty two-story in the suburbs, baking cupcakes and planning scrapbooking clubs, not stomping through overgrown vegetation to meet up with an operative like me.

I scanned her body looking for evidence of an injury but found none. She was also empty-handed. Worse, the wards were still up. "Forget something?" I shoved the enhanced night vision goggles that allowed me to see the pulsing magical wards on top of my head and pointed at the village. "Go do your job and bring those wards down."

She barreled into me with both hands, slamming her palms against my chest and shoving. I braced my legs to absorb the impact and caught her wrists before she could strike again.

"What kind of man are you?" Her whole body vibrated with righteous anger, but her voice broke.

I leaned close, baring my teeth in a snarl as I squeezed her wrists. "The dangerous kind." I let her feel the magic crackling over my skin. "You'd be wise to remember that, niñita, before I demonstrate it for you."

Rather than backing down like a sane woman, she bent forward and sank her teeth into my exposed forearm. I shook her like a rag doll, but she bit down harder, puncturing the skin with her blunt human teeth. She turned her head and spit a mouthful of blood on the ground before facing off with me again. "What kind of man kidnaps an innocent?"

I pushed her away from me and put some distance between us. "There are no innocents here." She might look like an angel, but even before she bit me like a feral kitten, I'd read her rap sheet. Innocent, she was not.

Mel followed me, digging a pale, pink-tipped nail into my chest as she raged. "Did you know the target wasn't an object?" She must have seen the answer on my face because she stepped away, drew her leg back, and stared at my groin, telegraphing her target clearly.

And fuck if that didn't make me hard. "I wouldn't do that if I were you," I warned.

She swung from the hip as she struck. Instead of blocking the shot with my leg, I grabbed her thigh and pulled her off balance. She crashed into me, so close I felt the angry tremors wracking her body.

"You knew." She packed so much despair into those two words that I released her. "That's why you wanted me to bring those wards down." She stumbled away from me, grabbing the disc from her pocket and tossing it at my feet. "So, you could walk into the village and kidnap a child."

I stilled, the blood pounding inside my skull. "What did you just say?"

Mel lifted those doe eyes to mine, pleading. "Tell me you're not the kind of man who harms a little girl."

Fucking Steve. I should've kept squeezing when I had him by the throat.

I bent close enough to Mel that our breath mingled. "I swear it. All I knew was that the vessel was a person. I had no idea it was a child."

All the fight went out of her. "I believe you," she whispered. Then, she put her thumb and forefinger between her lips and whistled, the sound shrill enough to make me wince.

Seconds later, we were surrounded by villagers armed with bows, knives, and clubs. I shoved her behind me. "What did you do?"

Of course, the little thief didn't stay behind me. Instead, she planted her fist in my kidney before side-stepping around me to greet the wiry, middle-aged man who was obviously in charge of this rag-tag group.

"This is him." She jerked her head in my direction while I struggled to draw in a breath from her cheap shot. "He says he didn't know," she said.

The man's eerie blue eyes were slitted like the devil as he studied me. "You trust him?"

Mel bit her lip. "I trust he didn't know we were sent here to take your granddaughter."

My gaze snapped to the man's. "Your granddaughter?"

"I have a proposition for you, Shadow." He gestured to a woman dressed in a long dark cloak, a scroll in one hand and a dagger in the other. "But first, I need your oath that you will see that no harm comes to my granddaughter."

Even surrounded, these villagers were no match for a Shadow. I should walk away. With the chalice already in my possession, I could easily hand it over to the Enclave and wash my hands of whatever clusterfuck this was.

"Keep your proposition. We're leaving." I grabbed Mel's arm and propelled her toward the beach, but she jerked free.

Mel scrambled to the man's side and lifted her chin. "Not without the girl."

"You've got to be kidding me." I stared at the two of them. "No one in their right mind would ask an assassin and petty thief to babysit their kid."

Mel's cheeks flushed. "I am not a petty thief." She held up four fingers. "Four counts of grand larceny and armed burglary, plus a front-page news article. The press gave me a nickname, you know. And that's only the heists they busted me for."

I raised a brow. "My point exactly."

"We can't leave her." She crossed her arms over her chest. "She needs us."

"Look, niñata. You want to play house, have at it. I've got shit to do and people to kill." I turned to leave.

"Child, no," the man yelled. "Get back."

A small girl who couldn't be more than three years old blocked my path, a riot of wispy blonde curls framing vivid blue eyes identical to those of the man. I stared down at her, waiting for the tears and terror to take hold when she got a good look at me.

Instead, she raised her chubby arms and tipped her head back. "Up!" she demanded, not a trace of fear in her small body.

One word, and my chest cracked wide open, her sunshine voice and earnest blue eyes burrowing past years of brutal training and ugly missions. Before I could stop myself, I lifted her into my arms.

And when she placed her soft palms against my stubbled cheeks and giggled, it became inevitable that I'd give this man my blood oath to protect this child's location with my dying breath. But I knew if I left her here, the next operative Cerberus sent in my stead would crush the light in those trusting blue eyes and turn her into someone like me.

In the end, both Mel and I cut our palms and signed our names to the witch's scroll, swearing we'd safeguard the child's location. When we finished, the witch brought down her wards. The man glanced at the little girl clinging to my neck, sorrow lining his weathered face before he looked away. "Follow me," he said. "There's something you need to see before you give me your answer."

The child rested her head against my shoulder, her curls tickling my neck, as I followed him through the village. When we stopped in front of a small cottage, she whimpered and clutched my shirt.

The man paused with his hand on the doorknob. "It's best if the child doesn't come inside. Too many bad memories." Even as he said it, he avoided looking at her as if she were tainted by whatever happened behind that door.

A big scowling man stepped forward to take the child from me. Her lip wobbled, and the crack in my chest widened. But she went to the man willingly, so I let her go.

Unlike the quaint outside of the cottage, the inside made my skin crawl. Beyond the food-encrusted dishes and slashed throw pillows strewn across the living area, the walls were covered in runes and notes straight out of a psychotic break. Someone had scribbled warnings in blood-red marker from floor to ceiling. Where the words stopped, hand-drawn scenes of flames and demons took over.

In the center of it all, my gaze locked onto the stuffed white dog marred by bloody fingerprints so small they made my breath freeze in my lungs. "What happened here?" The scent of death still clung to this place.

The man's fists clenched at the sight of the blood. "This is where my son was murdered."

Mel gripped my arm, her nails digging in. She blanched at the implication. "And the girl?" she whispered.

The man clenched his jaw. "We found it over there." He pointed to a corner of the room. "She must've huddled near Henrik's decaying body, clutching that stuffed dog. Rosa left him to rot for days while my granddaughter played nearby." His voice cracked like a whip with anger at his son's loss.

I picked up the toy, trailing a finger over the ruined fur. "Who killed him?"

"Her mother." He picked up a photograph showing a laughing young man cradling a baby in his arms. "She went by Rosa, but I don't think that's her real name. Whoever she is, she's a powerful witch, and she'll stop at nothing to get her hands on my granddaughter."

"The wards?" I asked.

"Yes." He sat the photo on the end table and pointed to the writing on the walls. "Rosa believed her child was the key to a demon prophecy. She's tried several times to steal her."

Mel and I circled the room, reading the mad scribblings. Some of them weren't legible, others incomplete thoughts written over and over. The words I could make out painted an ominous future.

They shall call forth demons
Only the strongest survive
Five breeds born of earth
Strike one
Strike them all
Sacrifice the child

Water and air
Destroy the vessel
Weaken the forge
His claim
In blood and bone

With the words burned into my brain, I was the first to leave that house of death. Outside, the girl sat alone, digging a stick into the hard-packed ground to draw images of a man and a child with wild hair. Her lower lip no longer wobbled, but her blue eyes were bright with unshed tears.

"What's your name, child?"

"Riley." She reached out and touched the knife tucked into my boot. "Ouch," she said like she knew what a blade felt like. She raised those luminous eyes to mine. "Are you a bad man?"

The faceless bodies of my kills whispered the answer, but I banished those ghosts to the nights I couldn't avoid revisiting them. "Only when I need to be."

"Who are you?" She stuck her thumb in her mouth, unconcerned with the dust clinging to it.

I bent down and lifted her out of the dirt. "I'm your ticket out of here, baby girl."

CHAPTER 20

A lot of things could be postponed in a crisis. Coven game night wasn't one of them. Despite how often it devolved into magical brawls, Helen insisted it built character. Between her competitive streak and her love of testing her latest potion bombs on live subjects, it was her favorite night of the week.

Because it was my turn to host, I'd selected a game that served double duty. I'd also expanded the guest list to include Volkov, Nash, and Dez. As an honorary coven member, Garth was already a game night regular.

Tonight, Helen set up his Ouija board beside a cocktail glass full of triple bug mix. When Circe ambled by, Garth puffed up to twice his size and brought out the spurs to guard his special chicken treats. Unimpressed, the cat flopped to her side and licked her butthole while maintaining eye contact with the disgruntled vengeance demon.

Helen shooed the cat away before turning to the game board aka chalk wall. She tapped the toe of her orthopedic sneaker while glaring at the wall. "That's not even a real game."

"Sure, it is." I pointed to the *Guess the Prophecy* I'd written in fancy chalk letters. "It's a puzzle."

"Puzzles aren't games," Helen argued. "They're activities."

Dez nodded. "Like golf." He grabbed a Twizzler from our candy buffet and chewed on the end.

Volkov ditched his suit jacket and scowled at Dez as he joined him on the couch. "Golf is definitely a sport."

Nash sprawled out on the other side of the couch in his usual ratty flannel and jeans. "If you ride around in a little cart and pay some kid to carry your clubs for you, it's not."

"The sport isn't getting to the green." Volkov caught my wrist and tugged me closer with a wink. "It's all in the stroke."

I let him pull me down for a kiss before settling on the cushion next to him.

Bea purred. "Finally, a man who gets it." She wedged herself between Dez and Volkov, sipping a fruity cocktail in a plastic flamingo cup. "Give me a man who can handle his wood, and we'll make it an all-night sport."

That was one way to kill the golf debate.

The tips of Nash's ears turned pink, and he coughed into his fist. Dez distracted himself by taking another bite of his Twizzler and ignoring Bea's nudge to his ribs. She loved to rile him up.

Volkov ignored all of them to brush my hair back and press his lips to the curve of my neck. "How long does game night typically last, anyway?"

Helen chucked a piece of chalk at us. "You're not tempting her to ditch game night early."

Alyce played coven referee before we got any more off

track. "Does your game involve magic, sweetheart?" she asked me. "Because that's the rule."

"Yup." I crossed my arms behind my head and gloated. "End-the-world magic."

Helen threw up her hands. "Fine. We'll play your made-up game."

To gamify our brainstorming session, we all rolled dice to determine who would go first. I won, so I recorded the lines from my father's latest memory on the chalk wall. Some of the phrases matched the snippet of prophecy Sato had grudgingly shared with us, but others were new. None of them were all that helpful on their own, but we had to start with what we knew.

When I finished, I grabbed a handful of gummy worms and plopped on the couch next to Volkov. "Your turn. Did you have a chance to talk to your brother?"

Volkov grimaced when I offered him a worm I'd already bitten in half. "That's disgusting." He also ignored the chalk. "I spoke with Aleksei this morning, but it was a dead end. According to my brother, rumors of Cerberus died out years ago. He ranks it up there with urban legends." Volkov dropped an arm around my shoulders and tucked me close in spite of my choice of snack. "He could be wrong, but I find it hard to believe a black ops unit could exist under Aleksei's nose without him being aware of it."

"Either it's a defunct group," Nash reasoned, "or it's operating outside the bounds of the compound."

"Or both," Volkov said.

I tossed Bea the chalk, and she drew a three-headed dog with a giant question mark above it.

"You're up, Dez," I said.

He wrote Bellarose's name beside Bea's drawing. "As you

all know, Zara Bellarose did a brief stint on the Witches' Council. I did some digging into the year and a half she was on it. According to the archives of meeting minutes—"

Volkov smirked down at me. "See, those meeting minutes are useful," he whispered.

I rolled my eyes. "Sure. To leave dirt for your enemies to dig up years later." We weren't about to start taking coven minutes, no matter how often Volkov tried to convince me that parliamentary procedure wasn't a snoozefest.

Dez cleared his throat to drag our attention back to the task at hand. "Like I was saying, Bellarose's contributions to the meetings were limited to inquiries about demon artifacts and illegal magic. From what I can tell, she was frequently at odds with the other council members. Although the minutes from the meeting where she was removed were light on the details, there were accusations that she'd regularly broken protocols, undermined council decrees, and attempted to wrest power from local covens, particularly those in Norway. The vote to remove her was unanimous."

None of that surprised me. From Olav's account, I already knew she'd made several attempts to smuggle me off the island as a child. And based on my father's memory, a witch erected the wards around the village. If Bellarose had managed to wrest control of the local covens, she could've ordered the witch to dismantle her own wards.

"When did she sit on the council?" I asked.

Dez jotted down the years she'd served. "Within a year of leaving the island, she'd secured her spot."

"She would've been what, early twenties?" Alyce looked at Helen. "That's unheard of."

"It is," Helen agreed. She squinted at Dez. "Was she elected?"

He shook his head. "No. Appointed by recommendation of the Enclave to fill a mid-term opening."

Helen stabbed a finger toward the wall. "You better add that to the game board."

Dez did as she asked. "Since she obviously had connections, I did a deeper dive into her background as well. Her birth certificate listed her parents as Rupert Bellarose and Francine Higgins. Francine died in childbirth, and I couldn't find any record of a second marriage for her father."

"Both witches?" Helen asked.

"There's not a lot of info on her mother, but Rupert Bellarose had a reputation as a powerful seer. His name popped up frequently as a consultant for the Witches' Council."

"That explains the connection, then," Volkov said. "Do you have an address for this guy?"

"That's where things get interesting." Dez adjusted his glasses. "Rupert was listed as a missing person when Zara was nineteen, and if my math is correct, that would've been right around the time she hooked up with Henrik."

"You think she's responsible for her father's disappearance?" I asked. From my interactions with her, she seemed capable of it.

"It's a definite possibility," Dez said.

Now that his turn was over, Dez picked up his laptop to check the camera feeds he was monitoring. Everyone else took their turn, adding any clues or intel they had about this prophecy or the players connected to it. Unfortunately, it didn't amount to much.

Garth crowed, reminding us that we'd skipped over him.

I soothed the rooster by petting his feathers and nudging

the Ouija board closer. "Sorry, bud. We didn't mean to skip you." As he pecked the planchette, I sucked in a breath. "Wait a minute. Garth, you're a high-ranking vengeance demon, right?"

He stopped pecking long enough to puff up his chest.

Helen scooted forward in her chair. "Do you know about this demon prophecy?"

Garth crowed. Then he moved the planchette to spell, "demon war."

Nash sighed. "We already know that. Do you actually have something useful to add?"

Garth launched himself at Nash's cowboy boots, spurs out. When he'd made his point, he marched to the board and moved the planchette to "yes."

Helen hand fed him a treat. "Can you tell us the full prophecy?"

Garth clucked and stomped on the "no."

I guess it couldn't be that easy.

"What can you tell us, bud?" I copied the letters to the chalk wall as Garth wrote, "blood moon."

Nash scratched his chin. "What does that mean?"

Garth's eyes burned brimstone red as he spelled, "When the veil will fall."

Nash frowned down at his roommate. "You sure about this?"

After a peck to the shin, Garth wrote, "I have sources."

"Oh, right. Watch out CIA, the rooster has sources," Nash scoffed.

Helen swatted Nash's arm. "Don't be a jerk. If my Garth says he's got intel, then I believe him."

Volkov scratched his cheek. "But how?" He glanced at the Ouija board. "Is he calling home with that thing?"

Garth clucked and shook his feathered head. He nudged the planchette with his foot to the letters for "Magic Paws."

"I knew it!" Helen cackled and slapped Nash on the back. "Admit it. Sending him to that vamp-run doggie daycare was a good idea."

Nash stared at the puffed-up rooster. "Fine. Doggie daycare wasn't a completely stupid idea."

Helen harumphed and mumbled about people not knowing a good thing when they stumbled into it.

Garth preened. He used his beak to nudge the planchette across his Ouija board.

We all watched the rooster spell out, "Who's Your Daddy?" Then, he tilted his little head and stared at Nash through hell-fire eyes.

Helen's lips twitched when Nash's face flushed as red as Garth's demon eyes. One look at each other, and Dez and I clutched our bellies, laughing until we were gasping for breath. Even Volkov smiled.

After the tension that had been riding me for days, it was as if a valve released. I wiped a tear from the corner of my eye and held my hand up for a feathered high five. Garth obliged, bumping my palm with his wing. When I looked down, the eyes of an ancient vengeance demon gazed back at me. I reached down and stroked his red and teal feathers. Our bonding moment was cut short when Garth snatched a gummy worm out of my other hand and waddled away to chase Bea's cat.

"Anyone know when this blood moon happens?" I asked.

Dez grabbed his laptop to search. He grimaced. "The next blood moon is in a week."

We all groaned.

I rocked back in my seat. "Maybe it's not this particular blood moon but one of them."

Garth shot down that hope with a firm foot to the "no" before wandering off again.

I rubbed my temple. "So much for having time to untangle all this." More than my life as the vessel was at stake here, and a week was not enough time. If the Enclave couldn't decipher this prophecy in the decades they'd been trying, how the hell were we going to manage it in the next seven days?

Volkov squeezed my shoulder. "We'll figure it out."

His words were reassuring, but by now, I'd uncovered all his tells. And the tic in his cheek said Volkov was as worried as I was about the timeline.

Helen picked up the chalk and marched to the wall. "Stop dilly-dallying then, and let's get to work solving this puzzle."

Everyone sat up straighter.

"Okay, here's what we do know," I started. "Bellarose is somehow connected to all of this. And we know when the vamps trying to bring down the veil discover I'm the vessel, they'll be gunning for me along with hunting the elemental child who disappeared."

Helen underlined the most damning lines of the prophecy from our notes on the wall and read them out loud. "Sacrifice the child who wields water and air, destroy the vessel, weaken the forge."

A growl shook Volkov's chest. "Simple solution then. If they can't get their hands on you or this kid, no demon apocalypse."

Our definitions of simple differed greatly.

"About that." Dez interrupted. "You know that mystery woman we keep seeing coming and going from Bellarose's penthouse? I finally got a clear view of her face." Dez flipped his laptop around so we could all see the security footage in front of her building. "She can't be older than early teens."

I took the computer from him and zoomed in. Hollow cheeks, darting eyes, and hunched shoulders under the cape she wore any time she left the premises. "That's her." Zero doubt. She had to be the missing elemental child. That would make her about twelve years old.

Nash swore. "That's why Bellarose installed all those new security features on the penthouse. It wasn't to keep us out. It was to keep the elemental in."

CHAPTER 21

"That's not all." Dez clicked through a few camera feeds until he hit the street cam he was looking for. An unmarked panel van with dark tinted windows was parked next to a building close to Bellarose's penthouse. "I ran the plates. The van's a rental." He pulled up an international driver's license next.

My stomach sank. "Romanian."

"Yeah," Dez said. "The guy is a low-level vamp who works for Wallace Ratcliff."

"Crap," I mumbled. As the master vampire, Wallace Ratcliff was top of the vamp food chain. Attracting his interest didn't bode well for any of us.

Volkov stiffened. "He's making a play for the elemental."

Dez clicked through a few time stamps showing the van in the same spot. "So far, he seems content to wait and watch."

"That's good." I rubbed my arms as I considered our options. "Maybe we're the only ones who know about the blood moon, thanks to Garth." If Ratcliff wasn't aware of the looming window to bring down the veil, he might not make a play for the girl before we could figure out how to extricate her.

Dez fussed with the collar of his button-down shirt. "Bellarose scheduled an auction five days from now. I doubt the timing is a coincidence."

"What's up for auction?" Volkov asked the question I couldn't force past my lips.

Dez's soft brown eyes were apologetic as they met mine. "The girl."

I dropped my head into my hands. "Damn it." Some small part of me had held out hope that the woman who gave birth to me could be redeemed. That a kernel of goodness remained under her madness. But if she was willing to auction off a child to a room full of vamps ready to slaughter her, Bellarose was rotten to the core.

Volkov dropped a hand to my shoulder, his thumb soothing the tense muscles. "Five days is plenty of time to come up with a plan."

"You're right." I took a deep breath. "First, we need to figure out exactly where Bellarose has the elemental locked down. Can we make an educated guess?"

"On it," Dez said.

"And we need to know who the interested parties are willing to bid on an innocent kid." Volkov's wolf made an appearance, amber eyes promising retribution.

"That too." Bloodlust turned my sweet friend's eyes vamp red as he got to work.

"I'll figure out a way Nash and I can bust the girl out." I switched into heist mode, mentally running through Bellarose's security, searching for the gap that would get me inside. There was always a gap.

The image of the child buried beneath a cloak as

Bellarose's guards shuttled her into the building spurred me on. The kid had mastered locking down her fear because her expression on that photo was perfectly blank. And I remembered the trauma required to craft a mask like that.

My head snapped up, and I squared my shoulders. "Dez, I'm going to need an untraceable phone. Once we have her, we'll split. I'll find a place to lie low with the elemental until after the blood moon."

"Not happening," Volkov growled, bracing for a fight.

I spun to face him. "Max, Bellarose is going to hit back. And the Enclave is going to come for this child the second they suspect we have her." I blew out a breath. "Going to ground is the only way I can keep her alive."

Volkov cupped my neck, drawing my attention to him. "You get her to Kansas City, and the pack will protect her." When I opened my mouth to object, to tell him that he couldn't force the pack to protect a witch, he dropped his forehead to mine, all the authority of his wolf in his voice. "I swear to you I will keep the child safe. Just come back to me."

"I'll call in favors," Helen promised. "You don't have to do this alone, hon."

Years of conditioning urged me to run. I latched on to Volkov's steady breathing, the cadence settling the panic in my chest. And I reminded myself I had other options. I could choose to be a fighter now. "Okay. We'll get her here and make our stand."

"That's my girl." Volkov's lips brushed mine in a kiss so soft it snuck past the last of my fear.

"Now get up." Helen grabbed a fistful of my shirt and hauled me to my feet. "You need to get better at stealing magic before you go up against Zara Bellarose again."

Helen marched across the room to where I'd stashed the

box of my parents' crystals. She lifted the next one, labeled with Amelia's name, and held it up as if she could glimpse the memory held within it. "Let's hope your mom left you a how-to manual in this one." She handed it to me, then clapped her hands to scatter the rest of our crew. "Janis, find out if your niece is in the mood for a little fire-bombing."

Dez widened his eyes and mouthed, "WTF?" I shrugged. I had a feeling we'd find out what that meant soon enough.

Helen jabbed a finger at Nash. "You take Garth home. It's past his bedtime." Sure enough, the rooster was perched on top of the flatscreen television with his feet tucked under his fluffy belly and his eyes closed. "You." She singled Volkov out next.

He arched a brow and crossed his arms. "I know how to handle my business, witch."

She muttered about wolves and their oversized egos. Everyone else scampered off to do her bidding, while she opened her grimoire and started to chant.

The memory came to me as if it were my own. I sat at the kitchen table in our Santa Fe rental house. Every detail of the room was achingly familiar—the chipped corner of our Formica table, the tacky goose wallpaper border, and the old white refrigerator covered in cheap magnets and priceless photographs of our life together.

I smiled as I watched Santiago build a Jenga block tower on the peeling linoleum floor with our bubbly four-year-old. He stacked another block on top, this one making the tower sway. Instead of crying at the impending crash, Riley roared like a lion just like he'd taught her and knocked the entire thing to the ground with tiny fists. Her dad scooped her up and tossed her in the air until she belly laughed. The sound lodged in my chest, and I smiled at Santiago when he caught my eye.

He sat her on the floor. "What should we play now, baby girl?"

She hopped from one foot to the other. "Tornado!"

I bit my lip. No matter how many times I watched Santiago use his magic to whip the wind into a funnel for her, it always felt like a risk. We'd kept her hidden for over a year now, but I knew better than to relax my guard. Her mother was still out there somewhere searching for her. If Rosa got her hands on our precious girl, she'd snuff out the sunshine Riley brought into this messed up world.

Sensing my worry like he always did, Santiago wrapped a gust of air around me like a hug. He grinned at Riley and reached for the sugar bowl. Riley giggled and held up her hands, knowing the drill. Santiago poured sugar into her cupped palms. Then, he gathered the air into a palm-sized tornado and nodded to Riley. She tossed the sugar into the vortex, and we watched as the crystalline tornado spun faster and faster in his hands.

They'd done this dozens of times, and it always ended with sugar strewn across the kitchen floor and a wide-eyed girl enamored with her dad's magic. But this time, she didn't just watch.

She reached for it, her eyes glowing bright as she stole the magic for herself. "Look, papa. I can hold the tornado, too!"

All the blood drained from Santiago's face as he stared at our daughter, controlling his elemental magic like it had always been hers to command. The new, easygoing Santiago was nowhere to be found in the harsh slash of his brows and the muscles primed to take out threats with his bare hands.

"What does this mean?" I whispered, watching my

daughter laugh at the tiny, sweet tornado she held in her palm.

"It means I need to lock her magic down before anyone discovers what she can do." He kept his voice calm, but those dark eyes went killer flat as they clashed with mine. "If anyone finds out, they'll make her their weapon—or worse—eliminate the threat she poses."

I pressed a fist to my mouth to strangle the cry. When I got a handle on my emotions, I asked him, "You can do that?"

Santiago brushed a lock of blonde hair off Riley's forehead. "I'll find someone who can." He let her keep his magic even as he planned the block. "And her memory, too. We need to wipe it all out and hope it stays locked down."

My pulse ratcheted up to fight-or-flight territory. "And if it doesn't?"

"I'll take out any threats that come for her." Determination stiffened his jaw. "And we teach her how to protect herself, so when the day comes that we aren't with her, she has a chance."

I watched her cheeks glow with happiness as she played. Maybe I couldn't teach her the things he could, but I'd find other ways to be her shield. "Okay. But we're not cheating her out of a happy childhood. We do it in a way that lets her be a little girl for as long as we can."

Santiago crossed the room to where I sat shellshocked on a wobbly kitchen chair as our world spun out of control. He dropped to his knees and rested his big palms on my shoulders. "I swear she'll have the best childhood we can give her. We'll make everything into a game. When she's old enough to need the skills we'll teach her, she'll have a foundation of happy memories they're built on."

Before I could respond, he stood up and held his hand out to her. "Come on, baby girl. It's time for bed."

Riley pouted but let go of the magic, the tornado fizzling out. "I don't want to go to bed, papa."

Santiago picked her up, tossing her into the air until she traded her pout for laughter again. "You have to get a good night's sleep because tomorrow, we're going to build our very own obstacle course in the backyard."

She squealed and clapped her sugar-covered hands. When they rounded the corner and could no longer see me, I let myself cry for the life we almost had.

CHAPTER 22

"*Y*ou're sure this is where we are meeting them?" Kali tipped down her shades and stared at the sign for Old World Occult and Curiosities. The shop had been closed for months, a for-rent sign gathering dust in the window.

"This is it." I peered through the front window. The light was on. All the crystals, potion ingredients, and books still neatly lined the shelves of the main shop area, but there was no one in sight. "Janis said her niece bought the place when she moved to Kansas City a couple weeks ago."

Kali pushed her sunglasses to the top of her head. "You mean rented?"

I shrugged. "Janis said she bought it." Rent on the storefronts in West Bottoms was a bargain compared to other parts of the city, but the old warehouses that housed those shops garnered a pretty penny when they went on the market.

Kali whistled. "Shadows must get one helluva retirement plan to afford an entire building down here."

Although the compound guarded the identities of their

Shadows, we both knew for a fact that Liv Monroe had worked as one. Not that anyone would guess. A wide-eyed, strawberry blonde from South Dakota didn't exactly fit the mold for a highly trained supernatural assassin.

"Did you know she moved here?" I asked.

"No." Kali sounded irritated as she pulled open the door. "And she's going to get an earful about that."

"Not while Janis or the girls are around," I whispered, closing the door behind me. As far as her aunt and the others knew, Olivia had spent the last few years as a singer on a cruise ship. I poked Kali in the back. "Hey, after we save the world from a demon invasion, do you think she'll come over for karaoke night?" Even though her cruise ship gig was only a cover, the girl must be able to carry a tune. I started planning a duet playlist in my head.

Kali laughed. "Probably."

We followed the voices to what used to be a storage room.

"Uh." Kali stopped abruptly in the doorway to take in the scene.

Liv grinned at us. "Grab a hoop and get in line."

Familiar faces packed the room, most of them witches from the other Kansas City coven. All of them faced the front, swiveling their hips to keep their hula hoops in motion.

Kali bent close. "Is that Ruth?"

I nodded, watching the seventy-two-year-old in a sparkling turquoise track suit move her hips to keep the hoop in the air. She was doing better than most of the witches around her. Alona had dropped hers three times since we got here.

"Get with the program, ladies," Liv hollered, never breaking form. Unlike the others, Liv's hoop was on fire, the flames dancing around her body as she showboated.

I grinned and handed Kali a hoop.

She held it away from her body and pointed to today's rockabilly ensemble. "Do I look like I'm dressed for hula hooping?"

Helen came up behind us. "Stop being such a baby." She shoved Kali onto the floor, the lack of traction on her ballet flats offering no resistance.

For the next twenty minutes, we dutifully wiggled our hips to the chirpy pop songs blasting through the speakers. Keeping those hoops in the air was harder than it looked, but by the end of the class, I'd mastered the skill.

"When do I get one of the fire hula hoops?" I asked Liv as the class dispersed.

"How about never," Kali muttered.

"Why not?"

Kali, Janis, and Helen all stared at me.

Liv winked. "Come back next time, and I'll hook you up."

I fist pumped. "Yes!"

Once the crowd cleared out, we got down to business. "How do you want to do this?" Liv asked, an ember sparking to life on the tip of her index finger.

"We don't have time for training wheels." I cracked my neck and rolled my shoulders. "Light it up."

The first few times I reached for her magic, I couldn't pull it to me. But after several tries, I was able to redirect the fire where I wanted it. Liv tossed me a pair of Kevlar sleeves with thumb holes, and I practiced wrapping the flames around my fist without singeing all the hair off my arms. Next, I learned how to shape the fire into a ball and sling it like a major league baseball pitcher.

By the time we left, I had a promise from Liv that she'd

turn up for our next karaoke night and a better grip on my ability to wield magic.

"Don't get overconfident," Helen admonished. "Zara Bellarose packs a lot more of a magical punch than a sweet twenty-five-year-old fire elemental like our Olivia."

Kali bit her lip. She'd seen Liv in action more than once and knew the kind of fire power she brought to a fight.

"I'll stay humble," I promised Helen.

Helen herded us out the door. "Good. Tomorrow, we can tap the last memory crystal and practice channeling the other elements."

"I'm afraid those will have to wait. We're hitting Bellarose tomorrow."

Helen narrowed her eyes. "Why the rush? That auction isn't for four more days."

"The closer we get to that auction, the heavier her security will be. Our best chance of rescuing the girl is to go in before Bellarose locks everything down for the sale." The idea of her auctioning off a human being made my blood boil. I didn't want the child in Bellarose's clutches any longer than absolutely necessary.

"You got a plan?" Helen asked.

"Working on it." I gave Helen a quick hug. "Volkov has a private jet fueled up and waiting. We'll head out early. You in?"

She huffed. "Of course, I'm in. The girls can stay here to organize the witches we recruited. I called in the favor Alona owed us. She'll be here with her strongest witches to guard the child when we get back."

"Can you get your hands on an illusion charm by morning?" I asked.

"Sure." She tilted her head. "How strong do we need it to be?"

"As strong as you can get. Actually, make that two," I said, as an idea took shape. I kissed her cheek before she could duck away. "Thanks, Helen. I'll see you in the morning." She'd delivered more help than I hoped. Now, it was my turn to recruit some muscle for our cause.

After grabbing lunch from the neighborhood food trucks, I went to headquarters alone. Some things were better handled without an audience. I locked myself in the first-floor office to make the call, choosing the sterile glass and empty desk over tainting our hang-out space with what I needed to do.

Nate Irons' broad shoulders, craggy features, and steady gaze broadcast dominance even over a video call. Nothing about the man was remotely approachable. As the alpha of the West Texas pack, one of the largest in the country, and the head of the North American shifter council, he was one of the most powerful shifters in the country. I'd wager few people called out a man like Irons.

I decided it best to ease into my ask. "Thank you for taking my call."

Irons' slate-gray eyes were shrewd as he sized me up. "It's good to see you under better circumstances than our last meeting. I'm glad to see you've recovered from the attack at the tournament."

The last time I saw Alpha Irons, my blood from a nasty gut wound soaked the ground, courtesy of a werewolf who had tried to bury a blade in Max Volkov's back.

Irons scanned the area behind me as if looking for Volkov now. "Knowing your mate as I do, I'm surprised he's left your side unprotected after that stunt you pulled."

Rather than bristling at the implication that I needed Volkov to play bodyguard, I latched onto that sentiment like the opening it was. "If you want to call saving Max's life a stunt—" I shrugged. "But I assure you I can protect myself these days." I held eye contact long enough to verge on insulting. "That wasn't always the case though."

Because Irons was one of the alphas presiding over the recent shifter summit in Kansas City, he'd no doubt knew a little about my history from Volkov's bid to change who could bring grievances in front of the council. Although Volkov kept the details vague, he'd made it clear that my adolescent years spent under my old alpha Carl's boot heels had been rough.

Irons dipped his head in acknowledgement. "I assume there's a reason for this call," he said.

"There is." I took a deep breath to steady my nerves. "Max told me you were in charge of the Southwest Tribunal when I lived in Santa Fe years ago."

"I was." Irons waited for me to continue.

"That means my alpha Carl answered to you back then."

Irons inclined his head.

"I'd like to tell you what my life was like in the Santa Fe pack before I ask you for a favor."

Irons leaned forward in his seat, his flinty eyes giving no hint about what he was thinking. "I'm listening."

Because I'd spent a decade burying those years so deep in my psyche that they could no longer define me, talking about that time didn't come easily. Sharing the specifics with anyone —much less a man I barely knew—made my stomach cramp and the words lodge in my throat. That was the thing about terror though. No amount of distance or logic lessened its grip on me when I dared to dredge those memories up.

I gathered my courage by staring at the grainy photo of the

young elemental child at the center of this prophecy. Flanked by Bellarose's armed guards, the girls' eyes were haunted in a way I understood all too well. I ripped open the wound for her sake.

"I'm sure Carl's reputation for ruling his pack with absolute authority was known beyond the city limits, as was his penchant for stoking purist sentiments. Unlike so many modern packs like Max's and yours, Carl's only exception to his all-wolves rule was me." I took a sip of my open can of pop, letting the bubbles settle my stomach. Then, I told Alpha Irons about the toxicology report from my parents' deaths showing they hadn't been conscious when the fire Carl set consumed them—a small mercy. And I explained how Carl had taken an orphaned twelve-year-old in and trained me to steal for him.

The more I talked, the more cracks formed in Irons' stoic expression. First, frown lines marred his lips, followed by pinched brows and a clenched jaw. By the time I paused for another drink, he wore a mantle of guilt from his failing to stop the abuse I suffered under his watch. But when he opened his mouth as if to apologize, I cut him off because I was only getting started.

"I want you to understand what it was like living in a house full of wolves who hated the very sight of me." I drew in a long breath, holding it until my pulse slowed, and I was ready to face my past. "Those four years made me a quick learner. At twelve, I learned what happened to people who crossed men like Carl when he forced me to watch him take apart his enemies—one limb at a time. At thirteen, I learned shifter healing meant it took a day for a bruise from a steel-toed boot to fade enough I could work the cash register in Carl's pawnshop. Not even a year later, he taught me that it took three days for a broken leg to heal enough I could go out on another job. I learned how to pop a dislocated shoulder back into the socket with a door jamb and an old sock in my mouth so they couldn't hear my screams. Because if they heard me, it always made things worse. So, I learned how to be quiet, how to fade into the background, how to keep my eyes on the floor."

I laid it all out for him, needing him to understand what unchecked power looks like for those unable to defend themselves. Over the years, I'd carried so much shame for the things done to me without my consent or control. Today, I laid all of it where it belonged—at the feet of a man who should've stopped it. Irons could have made a difference had he not chosen to leave governance up to a cruel alpha who cared nothing for the shifters in his keep.

I raised my chin and met Irons' gaze head on. "Do you want to know the worst thing about living with a dangerous wolf like Carl?"

Irons didn't venture a guess. I supposed he didn't know because big men like Nate Irons rarely were on the brunt end of it.

"A lot of people assume it's the violence. But that's not it. The worst part was the anticipation that consumed every waking moment I spent under that man's roof. Even Carl's good moods ticked like a bomb waiting to go off."

By the time I finished, Alpha Irons' eyes were mercurial, the predator that lived inside him fighting the man for control. I gave him a moment for my words to settle on his broad shoulders.

"I owe you an apology," Irons said, his voice as tight as the fists at his sides. "You were a child, and I failed you."

I dipped my head in acknowledgement, but his apology

wasn't what I was after. "While I appreciate the sentiment, Alpha Irons, sorry doesn't change the past." I lifted the black-and-white photo of the elemental child, holding it steady in front of the camera lens. "You want to make amends? Show up for this girl the way you should have shielded me."

Irons unclenched his jaw and uncurled his fists. "Whatever she needs, she'll have it. You have my word."

It would have to be enough.

CHAPTER 23

*W*e took off for Toronto armed with two of the strongest illusion charms money could buy and a budding plan to break the girl out from under Bellarose's nose. We didn't need to rent a hotel room when we landed because we weren't planning on being in Canada long enough to need one. Dez did arrange for a rental SUV while we were in the air.

"Let's go over the plan," I said. This was shaping up to be my best plan yet, and I was practically vibrating with excitement at the thought of pulling it off.

"What is the plan?" Nash asked, slipping brass knuckles into the pocket of his black combat pants.

I dug through my duffle bag to find the top I'd bought last night and tossed it to Nash. Thankfully, Bellarose's guards wore standard black combat clothes that were easy to source.

"I can take out as many of her guards as I can without raising an alarm," Nash offered, holstering his gun.

Dez stared at the outline of Nash's shoulder holster visible beneath his flannel. "Shooting up the place in downtown Toronto is bound to raise an alarm."

Nash smirked. "That's what silencers are for, my man."

"Not this time," I said. "Your job isn't to take out the guards, Nash. We'll leave that to Helen."

She beamed at me, loading up her favorite gray cardigan pockets with an assortment of potion bombs she'd brought along in a paper bag.

Nash scowled at the tiny woman who raised me. "Listen, you're one scary witch, but there are a lot of guards, Helen. How are you planning on taking them out? Ants-in-your-pants potion bombs?"

"Nah. But that's a solid Plan B," I admitted.

"What's Plan A then?" He glanced at my duffle bag at my feet. "Explosives?" he guessed hopefully.

"Even better." I bounced my feet and rolled my ankles, warming up my muscles as much as I could while sitting on a seat in a cushy private jet. We wouldn't have a lot of time once we hit the ground, and I needed to be ready to fight and run for this one. "This time, we're running a con rather than a typical heist—the classic Kansas City shuffle."

Dez scrunched his nose. "I have no idea what that means." He looked at Nash who shrugged.

"It's essentially a bait-and-switch," I explained, digging a cheap ski mask out of my bag. I rolled it up and put it on, not bothering to tuck my bright pink hair beneath it. "Here's how it'll work. We'll wait until it's dark out before I attempt to break in the back door of Bellarose's building, just like I did last time." I dug out a high-definition photograph next. "Only this time, I'll use the photo I had Dez alter yesterday. While it still resembles Bellarose, there are now enough anomalies that it'll set off the alarm when I try to use it to bypass her facial recognition system."

I held my hand out, and Helen gave me a fist bump and a "hell yeah." She'd already vetted my plan on the drive to the airport.

"Wait." Nash frowned. "Your big plan is to get busted by her guards?"

"Exactly. That's how a Kansas City Shuffle con works. You use your mark's arrogance against them." I grinned. One thing Zara Bellarose had in spades was arrogance. She made damn sure everyone knew she was the most powerful illusionist alive. "So, I'm going to give Bellarose a con she can bust." I tugged on a strand of pink hair poking out from my ski mask. "When she spots me trying to fool her system to get inside, she'll send her security force to apprehend me. She'll also lock the girl down— probably in a secure bedroom. And while Bellarose is gloating over besting me, you three are going to run the real con."

At my nod, Helen held up one of the illusion charms we brought along.

"Helen is about the same height as the elemental we're rescuing." I handed Helen a hooded cape. "We used the security cam photo of the girl to cast the illusion. As soon as it's go time, all Helen needs to do is slip the charm in her mouth and bite down. The magic will be released, and the charm will disintegrate. She'll have about an hour to stage her grand escape and lead Bellarose and the remaining guards away from the penthouse."

Nash ran a hand across his beard. "Won't the guards know the girl's still inside?"

"That's where Dez comes in. He'll hack into the electrical grid and bring it down. The whole block will go dark, but for less than a minute. Just enough time it's plausible for the girl to have escaped but not enough to make them check on her." I looked at Dez. I probably should've run that part past him earlier. "You can do that, right?"

Dez rolled his eyes. "I could've done that in middle school."

I gave him a thumbs up. "When the lights come back on, Helen will make sure the front security camera gets a good look at her face, and then she'll lead them on a merry chase."

Helen cackled. "I'm about to take one of her fancy armored cars for a joyride."

Dez nudged his glasses up his nose. "How are you going to get into her car without the keys?" he asked.

Helen patted his cheek. "You are such a sweet boy, Dez."

"I'm not that sweet," he grumbled.

"I know, hon. I saw the show you put on in those leather pants last time we were here." Helen ruffled his red hair. "But don't you worry about me. I'll hot-wire the car. It'll be like the old days."

Helen had lobbied to drive the getaway car since I took the job as the Enclave's retrieval specialist. She had nerves of steel, a lead foot, and a youth as filled with juvenile delinquency as mine. The woman was about to be living her dream.

"You sure Bellarose will go after Helen herself?" Dez asked.

"Oh yeah. No way she'll let her big payday escape, and she's too arrogant to trust paid guards to handle the situation without her. The winning bid for the elemental child is guaranteed to make her an obscenely rich woman." Never mind that handing the elemental over to the vamps would be a death sentence for an innocent kid and a way to bring down the veil. People like Bellarose didn't concern themselves with other people's lives, and they were delusional enough to think wealth would insulate them from the destruction of our world.

I turned to Nash. "That's where you come in. In the chaos, it should be easy for you to slip inside dressed as a guard." I handed him a second photo of Bellarose and waited for Helen to hand over the other illusion charm. "This unaltered photo will get you past the facial recognition scanner and into the penthouse. Once you locate the girl, convince her to bite down on that charm. It'll make her look like Helen. Then, grab the girl and escape out the back."

"And if she doesn't cooperate?" Nash asked.

"She'll go." Who wouldn't jump at the chance to ditch a death sentence? Plus, I'd been in her shoes, and I would've seized any opportunity to ditch Carl's pack. "If she hesitates, make sure she knows what Bellarose and the vamps have planned for her. Dez will park the rental car down the block from the back exit. As soon as he spots you and the girl, he'll bring down the grid again. This time, he'll leave it down. The blackout plus the illusion charm will provide plenty of cover for your getaway. The three of you will head to the plane. Helen and I will meet you there."

Nash's frown deepened. "That's a great way to bust the girl loose. But how exactly are you planning on getting out of there, kiddo? Because we're not leaving you behind."

I smiled because this was my favorite part of the plan. "When the lights go out the second time, I'll shift, headbutt the guards, and make my break. They never expect a goat." I'd been practicing my shift since I hooked up with Volkov. While I couldn't compete with the speed of his shift yet, I'd whittled my time down to a respectable twenty seconds.

Nash sighed, stuffing his pockets full of extra ammo and zip ties. "You sure you're up for this?"

I cracked my knuckles. "Let's go find out."

CHAPTER 24

One of the perks of being cuffed to a wooden chair in the security office was that I had the best seat at the watch party. The bank of monitors showed live feeds of the street in front of the building, both entrances and the main room of Bellarose's penthouse, and the windowless locked room where the elemental girl was being held.

I'd put up a token fight when the two guards wrestled me to the ground earlier after I set off the alarm. Mostly, I scratched and slapped like the two hulking guards expected from a girl like me. I even managed a pitiful sob when one of them pinned me with a knee to the back before slapping on the handcuffs. As far as I could tell, these two were run-of-the-mill human guards. They didn't smell like shifters, and I couldn't detect any magic on them. Bellarose probably opted to send in the muscle because she didn't want to risk me tapping into a supernatural guard's magic.

Now neither of the guards paid much attention to me, confident they had me contained. Instead, they were both glued to the street view monitor that showed Helen hijacking

Bellarose's sleek black Mercedes-Benz S-Guard. Although I wasn't really a car girlie, even I knew that baby would set you back half a million. I wondered how many innocent lives Bellarose ruined to be able to purchase it.

Thankfully, Helen's illusion charm worked beautifully. If I hadn't known it was her, I would've sworn the elemental girl was hot-wiring that ride. Helen rolled the window down far enough to flip off the guards swarming the car. Then, she gunned it, driving like she was a Hollywood star in an action movie. I tipped my chair, balancing on two legs while watching Bellarose and several of her guards pile into a nearby Escalade and race after Helen.

Everything was going even better than I'd hoped. This might be my best plan yet.

While everyone was focused on the woman leading the chase, I watched as Nash strolled into the building dressed identically to the two guards still watching the street view. I kept tabs on the guards from the corner of my eye, ready to launch a distraction if necessary. Believing the penthouse was empty though, neither of them glanced at the monitors showing the inside of the penthouse. They were too busy waiting for the boss to come back with the girl.

With a black ball cap pulled low over his eyes, Nash moved through the penthouse like he was doing a sweep. When he reached the locked bedroom, he unbolted the door and stepped inside. There was no audio on the video feed, so I couldn't hear what he said to coax the girl into leaving with him. Whatever it was, she didn't look convinced.

The second she raised her hands, I remembered the two not-so-minor details I forgot to account for in my brilliant plan—water and air. She nailed Nash in the chest with a fire-hose-worthy stream of water she drew from the pipes in the walls. Water seeped through the sheetrock as she pulled it to her with one hand. With the other, she gathered the air around her to propel the flow. Nash covered his face, staggering under the torrential blast as he fought his way toward her. It was like watching one of those weather reporters battered by a hurricane.

This girl had more power than most witches who'd trained their whole lives, but her control over the elements was volatile. Soon, the water drenched both of them, puddling on the floor and soaking the bed. She balled her hands into fists, trying to wrangle the wind and water under control again. Her lanky blonde hair blew back from her face, and water drenched her plain gray t-shirt and sweats.

Throughout the battle, her face remained blank, not a hint of fear or anger cracking her mask. And that, more than anything, made my heart ache. Twelve-year-olds were supposed to be over-the-top emotional. Their raging hormones practically demanded drama.

The girl's struggle to control the elements was all the opening Nash needed. He tackled her to the bed, flipped her on her stomach, and zip-tied her wrists behind her back. Times like this, that special forces training of his came in handy. Before the girl had a chance to react, he put the illusion charm in her mouth and shoved a palm beneath her chin, forcing her jaw shut to break the charm. The magic worked flawlessly, changing her into a carbon copy of Helen. Nash ripped a soggy pillowcase to fashion into a makeshift gag right before the lights blacked out again.

The adrenaline pumping through my veins supercharged my shift, shaving off at least five seconds. In my goat form, my legs were far smaller than my wrists, which allowed me to slip out of the handcuffs easily. Because the guards were as arrogant as their boss, they hadn't bothered to lock the door, so I rammed it open with my head before barreling into the street. Before the guards could give chase, I raced around the building and onto the less populated side street. I was out of the line of sight by the time the streetlights came on.

Almost home free. I hopped sideways to celebrate my escape, only pausing when I heard a car alarm blaring in the distance.

My happy hops ended abruptly when I saw the offender. With his messy red hair, black-rimmed glasses, and nerd attire, Dez was easy to spot. The man didn't exactly blend in. He staggered away from the car he must've set off as he waved his hands wildly to get Nash's attention. And as if that weren't enough of a neon sign signaling our illegal activities, Nash ran across the street with a gagged seventy-year-old struggling wildly as she bounced over his shoulder.

"Hey!" A woman in a dark uniform shouted with one hand on the open door of the van while holding a dry-cleaning bag in the other.

At first, I thought she was another of Bellarose's guards who'd spotted our kidnapping-in-progress. I wracked my brain for a good distraction to buy the guys some time. It wasn't until she lunged for me that I got a good look at the writing on the side of her van—Toronto Animal Services. Two armed guards couldn't catch me. I wasn't about to get hauled to the pound by an Animal Control Officer. I'd never live that shit down.

The woman dropped her dry-cleaning bag to the ground and left the driver's side door wide open as she ran around the van. She threw open the doors, exposing the sturdy cages installed in the back. Instead of attempting to race past her, which would only draw more attention to Dez and Nash, I slowed down.

When she reached for the loop pole she intended to snare me with, her back was to me. I lowered my head and speared her uniform-clad butt with my horns, using my momentum to toss her against those cages. Then, I ran for the getaway car, grabbing the abandoned dry-cleaning bag in my teeth as I passed.

My shift to human took longer than my earlier change. Unwilling to let Dez drive, Nash had shoved him aside and took the wheel, keeping to the side roads. He refused to look in the rearview mirror in the off chance he'd catch a glimpse of me naked as I shimmied into my stolen dry cleaning in the backseat.

Once I was fully dressed, I gave him the all-clear. "You can check your mirror now."

Nash did a double take when he saw the Animal Control Officer uniform I was rocking, but he didn't comment on my choice of wardrobe. "That plan went to shit fast," he said.

I shrugged. "We're all here, aren't we? Seems like it went pretty well to me."

Nash laughed, shaking his head and adjusting his side mirror. "I'm too old for this."

"Oh please." I knocked his headrest. "You're practically a baby compared to Helen. She's in her seventies, and she's out there speed racing across Toronto in a stolen armored car." I tucked my shirt into my too-big uniform pants. "Where's the girl?"

Nash jerked his head toward the back. "She's in the trunk."

I grimaced but shoved down the guilt because our first priority needed to be getting her out of Toronto in one piece. I squinted to get a better look at Nash's face through the mirror. "Did she give you a shiner?" The skin around his right eye was definitely darkening into a bruise.

Nash let out a long breath. "Yup. Nailed me with her knee when I tossed her over my shoulder to save her ass."

I grinned. "Scrappy. I like her already."

"Uh, guys, I think we better turn around." Dez waved his phone in the air. "I got a traffic alert that the northbound expressway is down a lane because there's a wrecked car on fire."

Nash's worried eyes met mine in the mirror. "That's the direction Helen was headed." He flipped an illegal U-turn and headed back the way we came.

By the time we reached the scene of the accident, Bellarose's Mercedes-Benz was surrounded by emergency vehicles and engulfed in flames. I searched frantically for a stretcher with a cardigan-clad body on it. But no matter how hard I looked, I couldn't find her.

I didn't wait for the car to stop before I threw open my door.

"Damn it, Riley. Wait," Nash yelled.

Dez grabbed my wrist, preventing me from jumping from the moving vehicle. With his vampire strength, he had an iron hold on me. This time, the sob that worked its way out of my throat was real. "Helen is in that car. Dez, I need to get to her."

He didn't let go. "Riley, no one could survive in that car. Look at it." His vamp-red eyes were already glazed with grief.

The last thing I wanted to do was look closely at the inferno. I gritted my teeth. "Don't say that. She has to be okay." I looked at Nash through the blur of my tears. "I need to get to her. Now." Even though we couldn't afford the attention it would draw, there was no danger in the world that could make me abandon Helen. Until I held her charred body in my arms, I'd never believe she was gone.

Nash pulled the rental car off the side of the road and put the hazards on. He was out of the car before I was. "Stay with the girl," he told Dez before closing the door. "If you spot any of Bellarose's people, get her to the plane. We'll find another way to Kansas City."

Dez stared at the burning car up ahead but nodded, his eyes glowing as brightly as the flames as he moved into the driver's seat.

Nash caught my arm before I could bolt for the wreckage. "Rushing in won't help anyone. Be smart about this. We need to work our way through the crowd without drawing too much attention." He ripped the ski mask off my head and traded it for his black ball cap, tucking my hair underneath.

Another car pulled in behind us, its passengers climbing out to rubberneck with the burgeoning crowd. I ignored all of them, glaring at the man still holding me back. "Fine. Now let go."

Someone in a black hoodie elbowed me in the ribs hard enough to bruise. I ignored that, too, because the only thing that mattered was getting to the woman who'd been my anchor for almost a decade. I prayed I wouldn't be too late, that I'd find her arguing with the ambulance staff rather than turning to ash in the blaze.

The thought nearly drove me to my knees.

A hand whacked me on the back. "That was the most damn fun I've had in years, hon. You should've seen that witch's face when she spotted her precious car going up in flames." She giggled, her dark eyes dancing with mirth from the hoodie cinched around her face.

That explained the elbow to my ribs. I reeled Helen close

and sagged with relief, my heart nearly beating out of my chest.

The rhythmic thumping cut through the buzz of traffic and conversations going on around us. I didn't have to turn around to know where it was coming from. Anyone who'd been bound in a trunk before recognized the sound of kicks to the trunk lid. And people were starting to whisper and stare at our rental car.

Helen pushed Nash out of the way and slid into the driver's seat with a twinkle in her eye. "Might want to get your gun out to shoot out some tires, sonny." She looked over her shoulder at Dez and me in the backseat and winked. "Buckle up, kids. Granny's got the wheel." Helen cackled like a loon and hit the gas.

CHAPTER 25

a four-hour flight wasn't nearly enough time to win over a hostile twelve-year-old elemental witch, but it's all we had. Nash had cut the gag off as soon as the doors of the plane closed, but the girl hadn't made a sound since he'd deposited her in the comfortable seat and buckled her lap belt with her arms still pinned behind her.

Both illusion charms had worn off before we made it onboard, so I got a good look at her. The girl was waif thin, with intense dark eyes and tangled dishwater blonde hair. Her t-shirt was rumpled and the gray sweatpants loose on her slight frame. She was barefoot, her unpainted toes curled into the carpeted floor.

I crouched down until we were on the same level. "We're going to take the zip ties off now, okay? But I need you to stay calm while we explain what's happening." I gestured to the rest of my crew. "I promise no one here is going to hurt you."

Her gaze flew to Nash's face, lingering on his newly acquired shiner. She smirked before schooling her expression into a stony mask that rivalled even Craig Ward's stoicism.

Beneath the brave face she was showing us, I recognized the signs of terror that girls like us learned young to bury deep. Her knuckles were white where they gripped the soft jersey of her t-shirt, and her breathing hitched every time one of us inched too close.

"We're in an enclosed jet about forty thousand feet in the air. Do not use your magic in here, okay?" If she did, I was prepared to siphon her magic, but I hoped it wouldn't come to that.

She nodded slowly, and Nash cut her loose. She rubbed her wrists and watched us.

"What's your name, hon?" Helen asked.

The girl pressed her lips into a thin line and said nothing. I sat down across from her and, after introducing all of us, I explained the situation. I didn't hold information back, outlining what we knew about the demon prophecy and her role in it as well as the auction Bellarose orchestrated to sell her to the highest vamp bidder. A vamp who intended to use her for a sacrifice to bring down the veil. Throughout all of it, her face showed no reaction, but her quickening pulse gave away her fear.

"You don't have to worry," I assured her. "We're not going to let that happen. We have friends in Kansas City who will help keep you safe once we get there. The hard part is over. All we have to do now is lie low for a week until the danger passes."

She didn't look convinced.

After a minute of tense silence where we all waited to see if she'd trust us, she tucked one foot under a thigh and sagged against her seat. She reached for the bottle of water Dez had tried to hand her earlier and took a long sip. Then, she cleared her throat. "My name's Sierra." Her soft voice came out scratchy, like it had been a while since she used it.

I smiled at her. "It's nice to meet you, Sierra."

She didn't smile back, but she didn't flinch away from my outstretched palm either. Sierra placed her hand in mine and shook it with a surprisingly firm grip.

"Do you have parents who are looking for you, Sierra?" Nash asked.

She wrapped her arms around herself, squeezing her slender biceps. "No. I don't know who my parents are." She rocked slightly in her seat.

Helen and I exchanged a look. I forced a sunny smile and let the topic drop. During the rest of the flight, Helen and the guys took turns plying Sierra with airline snack food and stories about Garth and Circe. None of them could get her to crack a smile, but she listened intently as they talked.

I texted Volkov to update him on our arrival time and asked him to meet us at headquarters with a few of his shifters willing to pull guard duty. It'd be well past midnight before we landed in Kansas City, and we were all exhausted after the day's high-octane adventures. Having a few well-rested guards would go a long way toward making us feel safe enough to sleep.

By the time we landed, Sierra had relaxed enough to drop her hands from her sides. She even added to the conversation occasionally. But she never smiled.

After the wheels touched down, I handed her an extra pair of lilac-colored sneakers I'd brought along. "Why don't you try these on. We can go shopping for your own clothes and shoes soon, but for now, you can borrow mine."

Until the blood moon passed, we'd be limited to online shopping for the necessities. In a week when this all blew over, and both Sierra and I were still alive, I'd take her to all my favorite West Bottoms' thrift stores. I reached over and squeezed Helen's liver-spotted hand, remembering how she and the girls had taken me on my first thrift store shopping spree. While sixteen-year-old me would've balked at them paying mall prices, the bargain hunting had come with a price tag I could accept as a gift. Plus, hunting through racks of old eighties clothes with Bea had been like a balm to my battered soul. They'd even bought me a vinyl record despite me not having anything to play it on.

Sierra's hand darted out to take the sneakers as if afraid I'd change my mind and snatch them back again. I dug my nails into my palm, furious at whatever conditioned her to react that way. The borrowed shoes were a size too big for Sierra, so we stuffed tissues into the toes to snug them up.

"Ready?" I asked when she had them laced.

She nodded and followed me off the plane.

Nestled in a bend of the Missouri river, the downtown Kansas City airport was popular with private corporate jets like the one we flew in on. And though it was late, and this airport was always far less busy than KCI, the silence that greeted us when we deboarded had all the hair on the back of my neck standing at attention.

"Something's not right," I whispered, slowing to watch for the threat I felt hanging in the air to materialize.

Nash and Dez stepped forward to flank me, putting Helen and Sierra at our backs.

"Act normal." Nash unzipped his light jacket for easier access to the gun in his shoulder holster as he scanned the area. "Up ahead, sniper on the roof to your left."

No way Bellarose and her guards could've beat us to Kansas City. Not with Helen driving us to the airport. That meant either she'd hired mercs to intercept us, or someone else with a vested interest was here. Since we were already in range of a high-powered rifle, and that sniper had plenty of time to take a shot, whoever it was intended to capture us alive.

"How do we take him out?" I asked Nash.

"Not only him." Dez's eyes flashed red as he angled his head toward me. "I count at least a dozen heartbeats nearby."

Maybe a couple of those belonged to airport staff, but it was the middle of the night, and the place was deserted. That, in itself, was a warning. I had a feeling all those heartbeats belonged to people here for us. We wouldn't make it to cover before they intercepted us, either. It was fight or surrender. The second choice wasn't a real option.

I mentally inventoried our weapons. In addition to his gun, I could count on Nash for at least a few blades. Helen, who'd donned her favorite cardigan again, never left home without a pocket full of potion bombs. The woman also had a wicked right hook. As a vamp, Dez had fangs and super speed in his favor, not to mention his vastly improved hand-to-hand combat skills. I had a demon dagger tucked into the duffle bag slung over my shoulder, and a heavy-duty curling iron I'd left in the bag from my last overnight trip.

We were so screwed.

None of that would be enough to hold off a dozen trained attackers. From the tension riding Nash and Dez, they'd already reached the same conclusion.

I could practically taste the magic in the air as the wards around the airport snapped into place. I'd seen the shimmery silver magical threads before. "There's at least one witch among them because we're now surrounded by silence wards." Not good. "Stay close to me," I told Sierra, keeping my voice calm despite my rising panic.

Now that the wards were up, faceless armed men peeled from the shadows to close ranks around us, cutting off any route of escape. Nash, Dez, and I formed a semi-circle around Helen and Sierra with the jet at our back. I dropped my bag to the ground and kicked it aside, bracing my legs for a fight we'd never win.

One man moved like a wraith across the tarmac, and the others fell in line behind him. At first, I didn't recognize him in those hooded combat clothes. I was used to seeing him in cartoon t-shirts and skinny jeans.

"Turn over the girl." There was no hint of warmth in Kage Sato's soft voice. He was all business tonight.

"Not happening," I shouted.

All those favors we'd called in did us no good here. I thought we'd have more time before he came for the girl, but given the shit show in Toronto, maybe it shouldn't be surprising we'd landed on his radar so soon. Whether the Enclave had been tipped off to our rescue mission or Sato was working with Zara Bellarose as we'd feared, he'd brought plenty of backup with him. Big, lethal men. Shadows.

Helplessness clawed its way up my throat, but I didn't have the luxury of giving in to it. When I was Sierra's age, I'd been too scared to fight. But those days were over. No matter the odds, as long as there was breath in my body, I'd never let them take her. I widened my stance and bent my knees. Then, I reached for Sierra's hand and laced my fingers through hers. "Stay behind us. We'll fight to keep you safe."

The squeeze of her hand was so faint I might have imagined it.

Sierra pressed closer to me and whispered low enough only we could hear her. "I can fight."

Everything in me wanted to say no, to spare her from the unwinnable fight we faced, but I'd lived with the cost of backing down too many years to deny her. Even a child deserved a choice. Both Dez and Nash stiffened at her offer. Before they could shoot it down, I stepped aside and let her join me, our fingers still tangled together as we stood shoulder-to-shoulder.

With the river beside us and the crisp night air around us, Sierra had a magical battery to draw from. Maybe if I could help her control her power, we'd have a chance, even if it meant exposing the abilities that could sign my death warrant. "We'll channel it together," I told her.

"I suggest you reconsider." Sato raised a hand, and a red dot appeared on Sierra's forehead. "Cooperate and no harm will come to any of you. But the elemental is under the jurisdiction of the Enclave, and she's leaving with me, one way or another."

"Jurisdiction," I spat. "She's a twelve-year-old girl, Sato. What is wrong with you?"

Sierra squeezed my hand again. "It's okay. I'll go with them."

I tightened my grip. "Sierra, no. You can't trust these men."

"I know. They've come for me before." She swallowed, her grip tightening. "But I don't want anyone to get hurt for me." I heard what went unsaid as loudly as if she'd spoken it. She thought her life wasn't worth our risk.

Sato stiffened. "I don't know why you ran away from the safe house, child, but this time, I'll make sure you're protected."

Another Shadow stepped forward, his easy swagger and

arctic blue eyes all too familiar. "We need to leave now before my brother gets here." Aleksei tilted his head toward the road.

I battered down the hope that rose inside my chest because I'd told Volkov to meet us at headquarters. By the time he realized something was wrong, it'd be too late to do anything about it.

When Aleksei stalked toward us to retrieve Sierra, Nash aimed his gun at him. "Silver bullets," he lied. "Looks like we're at a stalemate."

I wondered if Sato was cold-hearted enough to let Nash pull the trigger. Sato didn't give a signal for his guy to take the shot.

A fleet of black SUVs sped toward us and screeched to a stop behind them, the headlights illuminating the sheer number of men we were up against. Max Volkov launched himself from the first vehicle and slammed his brother to the ground with a claw-tipped hand. "Stay the fuck down," he ordered, his voice thick with alpha command. "No one's taking that child."

His shifters poured out of the parked SUVs, evening the odds. There were so many of them, it had to be every domi-nant shifter in the pack. Teagan gave me a finger wave.

"You all came," I mouthed, my heart so full that they showed up for us despite me not joining the pack.

Teagan nodded. "First unanimous vote in pack history," she shouted.

Another set of headlights pulled up behind the row of SUVs. Alyce, Bea, Janis, Kali, Liv, and Alona climbed out of Helen's station wagon. The girls spread out among the shifters.

Alyce marched straight up to Kage Sato and grabbed him

by the ear, giving it a sharp twist. "You oughta be ashamed of yourself, young man."

Sato raised a dark brow at the young man comment as he extricated himself, and another Shadow blocked Alyce from a second attempt.

Liv waved at a scowling man with a buzz cut across from her. "Hey, Grif. Glad you could make it. I've been dying to kick your vamp ass ever since Yankton." She lifted her flaming palms and grinned like a manic pixie.

"Olivia Jane Monroe," Janis shook her finger at her niece. "You better believe we are going to have a conversation about this later. I thought you worked on a cruise ship."

"I guess the cat's out of the bag." Liv formed three fireballs and juggled them in her hands with the flare of a street busker. "Oopsie."

Aleksei snarled but stayed on the ground. "You took an oath, Liv."

"And technically," she said cheerfully. "I didn't break it because everyone here guessed. But now that they've all met my ex-coworkers." She shrugged.

Sierra looked at me, eyes wide and lip quivering. "I don't understand why they're all here. These people don't even know me."

"Because you deserve to be protected," I said.

I was so grateful for everyone who showed up for this girl. But all the witches and shifters in the world wouldn't erase the red dot still aimed at Sierra's forehead.

"Call off the hit, Sato," I pleaded, praying he'd listen.

Sato didn't budge. "Can't do that. I have orders to bring her in."

Before I could argue the point, two giant bodies dropped

like rocks from the sky. The gargoyles planted themselves in front of us, spreading their stone wings to create a bullet-proof barrier.

As soon as we were shielded, Volkov ordered his shifters to take down anyone with a gun. "Bring me anyone you catch with a laser sight, and I'll handle them myself."

"Don't make enemies you can't afford, brother," Aleksei said.

Volkov snarled. "Anyone who points a gun at a defenseless child was already my enemy. After Anya, you should feel the same."

I didn't catch Aleksei's response, but I could imagine how hard that hit. Their sister Anya died from a bullet meant for their father.

Once the threat was gone and the guns confiscated, the gargoyles lowered their wings and turned around. I wasn't surprised to see Craig Ward, but the other man shocked me. I'd assumed the alpha was a werewolf.

Nate Irons dropped to a knee in front of Sierra and tapped his fist to his chest. "No one will harm you under my watch."

Before I could thank Irons for keeping his word, Volkov strode toward me with his wolf in control. I met him halfway, wrapping my arms around his middle and leaning my cheek against his solid warmth. "I'm so glad you made it before they could take her." The fear for Sierra dissipated now that he was here with me. "How did you know we were in trouble?"

"The second the Shadows arrived, the shifters I had watching the airport alerted me. I got here as fast as I could." He let me go, and we turned to face his brother and Sato as they approached.

"No one would've hurt the child, Maxim," Aleksei frowned at Sato when he said it. "Kage was bluffing."

Volkov's wolf stared out at him. "I'm sure that'll console the traumatized child who had a gun aimed at her head."

"This isn't over," Sato warned. "We'll keep coming until we have the girl."

Helen elbowed her way past the guys, cocked her hands on her slim hips, and lifted her chin. "You come for one of us, you come for all of us."

"It doesn't matter," Sato said. "There's only one way this ends—with you handing her over."

"No," Aleksei said. "Maxim's right. I won't be a part of this. And neither will the Shadows as long as I'm in charge of the Compound."

For the first time since I met him, I saw raw emotion on Kage Sato's face. In an instant, the softness was gone though.

Sato didn't react when Aleksei and his men walked away. "The Enclave won't stop until they have that child locked down. She's too dangerous to walk free. If the demons get their hands on her." Sato didn't finish the thought. He didn't have to.

"They won't," I promised. "I'll keep her safe until after the blood moon and the demon threat is over. Then, she can have a normal childhood." She deserved one.

If Sato was surprised that I knew the timeline we faced, he didn't show it. He sighed. "If only it were that easy. Three days from now, the veil is coming down whether the vamps have the elemental child or not. But without her, the Enclave won't be able to stop them. She's the key. Think about what's at stake, Riley, and make the smart choice to hand her over."

Sierra joined us in time to hear Sato's words. She kept her eyes downcast and her expression blank as she waited for my response. I reached out a hand and held my breath until she took it.

Sato blocked our path. "Riley, what are you going to do?"

"Looks like we're going to save the world." I held Kage Sato's gaze. "But first, I'm cutting out the middleman."

CHAPTER 26

With the Enclave, Bellarose, and the vampires all itching to get ahold of Sierra, we decided to turn headquarters into a stronghold. Helen and the girls showed up bright and early the next morning with a station wagon full of air mattresses for our makeshift dormitory on the third floor. And good thing, too, because we were overflowing with guests.

Nash drove home last night to pick up Garth and, along with Dez, moved in temporarily to help keep watch. Alpha Irons refused to leave until there were no remaining threats to Sierra. He and Craig took turns perching on top of the building to guard from any skyborne attacks. Volkov organized a rotation of shifters so that at least four would be onsite at all times.

Liv and Kali brought donuts, hula hoops, and pets. Not only did we have a building full of people, we also had a rooster, a Chihuahua, a cat, and Liv's pet packrat loose on the premises. The place was an absolute zoo.

Which is why I left Sierra in Bea's care while Helen and I went to her house to tap into the last of my parents' memories. If I was lucky, there would be something stored in the tourmaline crystal that could help me face the coming demon invasion.

By now, Helen didn't need the grimoire to perform the memory retrieval spell. I made my blood offering and dove into the last of my father's memories.

The early morning air was cool off the mountains, and the sun sat low on the horizon as I took up a familiar position in the backyard. Our rental house wasn't much, but it had a solid adobe wall around the yard that afforded us much needed privacy.

Normally, I performed this routine later in the day with Riley, going through the motions like a meditation. But after tamping down my magic for months, I needed this outlet. Ever since I locked down Riley's powers, I hadn't let her see me practicing my elemental magic. To her, the movements were like Tai Chi—something relaxing we did together.

This morning, I was alone. I gathered the air to my palms and moved through the positions. My power built until it crackled like static electricity along my skin. I went on the offense, pushing air in a straight blast that would knock a grown man off his feet. Then, I whipped up a vortex strong enough to trap a small group before flattening it. More than once, I'd relied on that move to crush attackers. With a flick of my wrist, I pulled a thin current of the breeze toward me like collapsing a man's lungs.

Because air was my element, I worked with it exclusively. But water, fire, earth, or air—the movements to wield them were the same. Call the power to me. Build and release.

I practiced until the sun rose above the adobe walls and the light came on in the house as Amelia bustled around the kitchen cooking us a hearty breakfast. When Riley's voice drifted through the open window, I let go of my power, feeling the loss as keenly as a missing limb. I closed my eyes to ground myself. Then, I joined my girls in the kitchen, rolling tortillas filled with sausage, eggs, and a generous helping of green chilies.

The smell of homemade breakfast burritos lingered in my nose as I came out of my father's memory. Even mourning the loss of green chilies and lazy breakfasts with my parents, I felt lucky to have had as many mornings as I did with them. Just like my papa, I closed my eyes, grounding myself in a world without them. And I opened them again holding tight to the gift he gave me, the kinetic memory of how to wield other people's magic.

"Did you learn anything helpful?" Helen asked hopefully.

"Yeah. I did." I told her all about the vision over glasses of orange juice, toast, and scrambled eggs smothered in hot sauce.

We were finishing the dishes when Bea called. "Sierra had an accident. We were practicing her magic, and it got away from her. She flooded the whole first floor. I reassured her it was okay, that we could clean it up, but she freaked out, Riley."

I handed Helen her keys from the table and headed out the door as I talked. "Is she okay?"

"She locked herself in the panic room, and I can't get her to come out."

"Keep trying. I'm on my way." I climbed in the passenger side of Helen's station wagon.

"Headquarters?" Helen guessed.

I buckled my seat belt. "Yes, but first, I need to make a stop. Can you swing by the home improvement store?"

"Sure, hon."

Bea had managed to talk Sierra into venturing out of her hiding place by the time we arrived, but the girl looked terrified.

"Hey girls!" I called. "Come see what I got." I walked through the ankle-deep water in the first-floor bay without looking down.

I put my new wet/dry shop vac on top of the filing cabinet in the office. It was a good thing the high-tech door hiding our arsenal was waterproof. I took off my water-logged shoes. Next, I dumped out the contents of my plastic bags on the desk. Unable to resist her curiosity, Sierra moved closer.

"You want unicorn floaties or dinosaurs?" I asked her, pointing to her choices.

Sierra stared down at the assortment of pool toys with a wrinkled brow.

I picked up a beach ball and tossed it to Bea. "Put all that hot air to good use for me and blow this up."

Bea slapped my arm in mock outrage before starting to blow up the deflated beach ball.

"Better hurry," I urged Sierra. "Before all the good ones are gone."

She bit her lip as she chose the unicorn floaties like I'd expected. She didn't realize it yet, but her days of being stuck in gray clothes and a sterile room were long gone. The dinosaur floaties, I took for myself. Instead of blowing up the toys with our lungs, I talked Sierra into using her magic to inflate them. I slid mine up my arms and waited for her to follow suit.

"Hmm." I surveyed the office floor with its receding water-line and closed the door. "We're gonna need more water to test these."

Sierra sputtered, her eyes bugging out. Eventually she gave in and, with my help, pulled the water from the main bay area under the office door. When it reached our bellies, I kicked up my legs and floated around the office on my back. It took a little convincing but soon enough Sierra was frolicking in the water along with me and Bea. We bounced the beach ball between us with our fingertips and taught her how to play Marco Polo.

"What the hell happened here?" Volkov's deep voice carried through the office glass as he trudged through the water left in the main room toward the office.

Sierra froze.

Volkov opened the office door, and the water leveled out. When he saw the fear on her face, he looked like he'd taken a punch to the gut. Sierra began to tremble, too scared to dart past him. He let out a heavy breath and reached behind him to close the door. Without a word, Volkov removed his Italian loafers and his suit jacket and tossed them in the corner. He plucked the circle floatie off the coat rack where I'd hung it and put it to his lips.

Once he finally got the thing inflated, he slid it over his head, but he couldn't force his broad shoulders into it. He tried again, this time stepping into the floatie and pulling it over his soggy dress pants. It took a lot of wiggling, but eventually he stood in the middle of the office with an inflatable duck around his waist.

He'd never looked hotter than he did at that moment.

Sierra's face broke into a small smile. Volkov's answering grin was positively beaming. While Bea teased him about being a wereduck, I took a photo of all of us for the group chat. Then, we asked Sierra to fill the office with water again, and we spent another hour playing in it. We had three days before the world could end, and I couldn't imagine a better use of our time.

CHAPTER 27

The next morning, Sierra asked if she could come with us when Volkov and I went over to his place. Before I could object to the idea as too dangerous, Volkov had already arranged for an armored vehicle and a contingent of shifter guards rivaling a Secret Service escort. While we headed for his library to grab as many books on demonology we could carry for our all-day strategy session at HQ, Volkov encouraged Sierra to explore his home like it was hers.

She worried her lip with her teeth as she stared at him undecided, but he gently nudged her into motion.

"There are snacks in the kitchen." He winked at her and pointed to me. "I have to keep it stocked so this one doesn't get hangry."

I laughed. No lie there.

Six trips loaded down with books later, we found the kitchen empty. My palms grew sweaty, and my pulse raced at the thought of someone making it past the shifters guarding the perimeter to get to Sierra. The alarm didn't go off, but I, of all people, understood how easily someone who knew what they were doing could slip past even a state-of-the-art home security system.

"Hey. I'm sure she's fine." Volkov dropped a reassuring hand to my shoulder before my fear spiraled. "If she's anything like you, she's probably testing out my bidet right now."

I was too scared to laugh, but I managed a wan smile as we moved to search the rest of his house. The sound of a piano key halted us in our tracks. I sagged with relief.

"See? She's fine."

I followed him into the music room where Sierra gazed at the black Steinway grand piano with such wonder, her fingertips stroking the ivory keys.

"Do you play?" Volkov asked.

Sierra startled, clasping her hands behind her like she'd been caught doing something she shouldn't. "No." Her gaze flitted to the open door, then the window, cataloging her escape routes. "I'm sorry I touched it. I've never seen one except on tv."

Volkov snuffed out the growl building in his chest and hunched his shoulders as he approached her like he would a skittish animal. He stepped around her and slid onto the bench seat, patting the spot next to him. "Come here. I'll teach you how to play a song."

He held himself statue still while he waited to see if she would join him. And when she perched on the seat beside him, his body eased. Volkov positioned her hands on the keys and guided them with his own, the slow notes of "Mary Had a Little Lamb" filling the room. A genuine smile lit Sierra's face as she gave herself over to the music.

The vision of the two of them with their heads bent close together and their fingers dancing across the keys would stay with me, a new memory as strong as those my parents left me.

When we made it to headquarters an hour later, everyone else was already gathered in our fourth-floor team meeting space. Even with a giant sectional and an assortment of pub tables, we didn't have nearly enough seating for all the bodies in the room.

"Let's grab whatever chairs we can find on the other floors and bring them up here," I suggested.

"No need," Alyce said, drying her hands on her apron after mopping up a spill on the bar top. "Bea offered to pick up some extra seating."

I glanced at the shifters milling around my space and cringed, imagining what Bea might drag in. "I hope she doesn't show up with a dozen sex swings."

Sierra tilted her head to look up at me and crinkled her nose. "What's a sex swing?"

I froze, unprepared to explain that one to a twelve-year-old. Volkov made a beeline for Alpha Irons. Coward.

Alyce saved me, explaining its purpose matter-of-factly. Thankfully, Sierra didn't ask any follow-up questions.

Bea returned a few minutes later with a neon green beanbag in her arms. She recruited Volkov's shifters to carry in the rest, along with the books we'd packed in Volkov's trunk. In all, Bea had scored ten beanbags in an array of colors. The room looked like the fallout from a Skittles explosion.

I bumped her hip. "I freaking love it."

"Just wait until I make that man sit on one of them," she whispered before gliding over to Alpha Irons' side. The brief flash of horror on his face as she pushed him toward the hot pink sparkly one had both Sierra and me giggling.

Everyone took seats around the room. Dez, Nash, and the girls camped out on the sectional with Kali. Because Nate Irons insisted on being part of this planning session, we had two gargoyles in the room. Normally, they steered clear of each other since gargoyles were notoriously territorial. But despite gravitating to opposite sides of the room, both Irons and Craig Ward refused to be left out of something this important. Teagan volunteered to keep watch outside with a small group of shifters.

Unlike our usual close-knit brainstorming sessions, we had a room full of outside expertise to draw on. I hoped it would be enough to figure out how we were going to stop the demon invasion in the sixty hours or so we had left on the clock.

With no time to waste, I strode to the chalk wall to get started. Sierra followed me, tugging on my sleeve before I could address the room.

"I can go downstairs," she whispered. "Get out of the way."

"You have as much at stake in this as we do, Sierra. You don't have to be part of this if you don't want to, though. It's your choice."

Several people stiffened when they heard what I said. I raised my voice and repeated it to drive home the point. "I don't care what the prophecy says about Sierra's role. No one will force her to do anything she doesn't want to do."

Unshed tears welled in her dark eyes, but she blinked them away and lifted her chin. "I want to help."

"Then you'll help," I said. "There are a couple beanbags open. Pick whichever one you want."

Before she could sit on one of the remaining bags, Alpha

Irons offered her his seat, trading it for one of the open pub chairs before Bea could object. When everyone was settled, I picked up the chalk and wrote a checklist on the wall. *Decipher Prophecy. Save the World. After Party.*

Several of the men, including Alpha Irons, exchanged worried looks, but Volkov nodded for me to go on.

"Alright. We have two-and-a-half days to find a way to stop the vamps from opening the veil between our world and the demon realm. Here's what we know." I gave everyone an abbreviated recap and pointed to the pieces of the prophecy we did know. "First up, we need to get our hands on the rest of that prophecy. The obvious place to hit is the Enclave."

Low murmurs carried through the crowd. What I suggested was akin to treason, but all options were on the table as far as I was concerned. Before the objections could swell and drown me out, I kept going.

"The problem, of course, is that the Enclave's location is a closely guarded secret. Without that information, there's no way to steal the prophecy from their keep."

Liv raised her hand, fire sparking on the tip of her index finger.

Helen marched over, licked her thumb and forefinger, and snuffed out the flame. "Not in the house."

Liv mumbled "sorry" before turning to Kali. "Lucky for us, we have someone with insider information."

Kali was already shaking her head though. "I can't speak of the prophecy or the location without breaking my blood oath."

We all knew the consequences for that—instant death. Craig crossed his big arms over his chest and glowered at Liv.

She smiled at him but directed her answer to Kali. "You

might have taken a blood oath, but that demon inside you didn't swear one."

Finally. A woman who appreciated a good loophole as much as I did.

Kali sat up straighter. "You're right. Raum saw everything. And there's nothing stopping him from reciting the whole prophecy word-for-word."

"It's too risky," Craig argued. "He won't cede control if you let him take over."

"Hello." She tapped his cheek. "If I don't do it, he'll be the least of our problems when all his buddies swarm through a rip in the veil."

"What if Kali was in a salt circle when she called him?" I asked. "He'd be contained like any other summoned demon." I resisted the urge to tease Nash about his circle casting, holy water days. Now wasn't really the time. "Worse case, Kali's stuck in the circle until he gets bored or we call in enough magical firepower to wrest control away from him."

"It's too risky," Craig repeated.

Kali scooped her dog off the floor and settled Junior on her lap. "We don't have any better options."

Craig closed his eyes. "Fine. But I'll be in that circle with you."

"I know." She leaned her head against his shoulder.

Helen grabbed the container of salt and a can of spray adhesive she'd stashed under the bar for emergencies. She clapped her hands. "Come on, then. We can cast the circle in front of the karaoke stage downstairs." When several shifters stood up, Helen waved a finger in the air. "Necessary participants only. That means the witches in the room and Craig. Everyone else stays here."

Garth hopped on the coffee table and crowed. Helen made

a detour. "And Garth," she amended. The rooster wiggled his fluffy butt before launching himself at her, landing on her outstretched arm like a hawk.

There were a few grumbles but no outright mutiny among the rest of the crowd. Of course, Volkov ignored Helen and followed me downstairs.

CHAPTER 28

*A*pparently, Raum disliked the Enclave even more than I did, which made him surprisingly cooperative for a demon. Less than an hour later, we were all upstairs again with the missing pieces of the prophecy transcribed on a napkin Alyce found in her purse. We skipped over the beginning of the prophecy since Kali had already fulfilled her role in it and focused on the parts yet to play out.

Because Bea had the most legible handwriting, she copied it onto the chalk wall. Then, we tackled it in sections. The first part was the easiest to decipher.

On earth, their power is bound in fives.

In brimstone, we fashion our weapons.

Most of the demon weapons I'd retrieved with the exception of the blade I carried were in the Enclave's possession. I circled the number five with blue chalk and moved on to the next verse.

Be wary of the signet and the flame honed in blood,

And of the realm walker born of brimstone,

an unnatural alchemy to seal the veil.

"Any guesses about what any of that means?" I asked the room.

"Signets are rings, right?" Helen asked. "Could it be the ring your mother left you?"

"Possibly," I agreed, writing it on the wall with a question mark.

Garth jumped up and down until Helen got his Ouija board for him. A couple shifters scooted away from him when he started to move the planchette with his little foot.

"Is that like rooster Braille?" someone in the back of the room asked.

Since it was bound to come up sooner or later, I told them about the vengeance demon trapped in Garth's body. After that, even Alpha Irons gave the chicken a wide berth. The only one who seemed unperturbed by the news was Liv.

Garth wrote "me" on the Ouija board and clucked excitedly.

"Of course, he's the realm walker," Nash said, shaking his head.

Garth was clearly picking up habits from Circe because he rubbed against Nash's leg like a cat. Nash shooed him away, yanking his finger away when Garth's peck drew blood.

I stared at the words chalked on the wall until one of the pieces clicked into place. Pulling out my demon dagger, I held it up and pointed to the translucent stone in the center with flickering hellfire inside. "The flame honed in blood."

Dez leaned forward in his seat. "When we killed Mateo with that dagger, it soaked up his blood."

I nodded.

"Wicked," Liv said. "Can I hold it?"

Maybe it shouldn't be surprising that a fire elemental wanted to check out real hellfire, but her enthusiasm made more than one of the shifters give her the side eye. I flipped the dagger and handed it to her hilt first.

We moved on to the next part of the prophecy.

For if they acquire our weapons and unite the elements,
if they assemble the five breeds born of earth and
call forth the crone and the guardians
of stone and sky, human and hellfire,
they shall stand against us under the blood moon.

"Again with the fives," Helen said, scratching her chin. "Witch, shifter, vampire, necromancer, and human—the five breeds born of earth."

"And the crone?" Alpha Irons asked.

"Helen," several of us called out at the same time.

She preened as much as that rooster. "Obviously," she agreed.

Determining who might be the guardians took more discussion, but in the end, we decided the gargoyles accounted for the stone and sky reference, Nash filled the human slot, and Garth claimed the guardian of hellfire spot on the roster. The blood moon was self-explanatory as was the rest of the prophecy.

Strike one to strike them all.
Sacrifice the child who wields water and air,
destroy the vessel, weaken the forge.
He who brings down the veil shall reign as king of kings,
His claim written in blood and bone,
And demonkind shall again darken the world.

Although outing myself as the vessel and Sierra as the dual elemental felt risky, everyone in this room had earned the right to full disclosure, so I told them. As I finished, a man in the back of the room stood up. I'd assumed that he was one of

Volkov's shifters when he'd walked in mid-discussion wearing a hooded sweatshirt. When he dropped the hood, I stiffened.

"Impressive," Kage Sato strolled to join me at the front of the room like he'd been invited. He dropped a heavy canvas bag on the floor before studying the prophecy written in chalk across the wall.

Volkov leapt to his feet with a growl, and everyone closed ranks around Sierra.

Sato ignored them and kept reading. "Everything is in fives," he began, "which means stone and sky aren't likely referring to two of the same creatures.

"If not the gargoyles, then who?" I might be irritated to see the man here, but I wouldn't pass up an opportunity for intel even if he was the one to deliver it.

"The stone guardian is definitely a gargoyle, but I believe the guardian of the sky refers to me."

"And what are you?" Alpha Irons challenged.

A few people ventured guesses, none of them flattering. Liv sat on the edge of her seat, staring intently at the Shadow, more invested in his big unveil than even I was.

Sato crossed his skinny jean clad ankles and leaned against the wall. "Dragon."

"Hmph," Helen tossed an ants-in-your-pants potion ball at his head. "That's for threatening my Sierra."

Sierra sat up straighter when Helen claimed her as one of her own.

Sato didn't so much as flinch as Helen's magic went to work, but I smiled because—reaction or not—he'd be feeling the after-effect of that one for a while. When she hauled back her arm for a second attack, Sato held up his hands in surrender.

Helen hurled it at his head anyway. "And that's for the rest of us."

The room egged her on, but Helen left the rest of her potion bombs in her pocket, satisfied with her pound of flesh. For now.

With a room full of protectors, Sato wouldn't be walking out of this room with Sierra, so there was no harm in hearing him out.

"Why are you here?" I asked.

He looked at Sierra and then at me. "Because she carries the power to command two elements and, thanks to the call I got from Zara Bellarose, I know you are the vessel that will unite all the elements to seal the veil." Sato opened the canvas bag and began unloading demon weapons, lining them up on the bar top. "I brought the weapons, you already gathered the guardians, so all that's left is the fight."

Just because we had a goal that united us didn't mean I forgave what he'd done. I stalked past his array and retrieved my own demon dagger. With blade in hand, I leaned close to the man who'd pointed a gun at Sierra as surely as if he'd aimed it himself. "Hurt her, and I'll slay you myself, dragon."

Sato inclined his head and held out his peace offering—a signet ring. "The last piece of the puzzle," he said. "The Seal of Solomon. If the vampires succeed, the only way to bar the demons from our world is to infuse this with the elements to seal the veil."

We had almost everything we needed to stop the vampires from opening the gates of hell. Everything except the location where they'd attempt to bring down the veil.

CHAPTER 29

Barbecue was my favorite foreplay. And the buffet of smoked meats, baked beans, potato salad, and pickled vegetables spread across Max Volkov's kitchen island had me licking my lips and moaning like a porn star as I sampled them.

After spending the last two days strategizing our plan, practicing combing elements, and scouting potential locations for the apocalypse, we'd earned some alone time. Volkov and I left Sierra in Helen's capable care at headquarters, so we could spend our last night before the showdown together at his place. He'd ordered the food from my favorite hole-in-the-wall barbecue joint as a surprise.

If the world was ending tomorrow, this was how I wanted to go out—with a dangerously sexy man, Kansas City's finest barbecue, and enough time to savor both.

Volkov took off his suit jacket and rolled up his sleeves before piling brisket on a bun and setting it on my now empty plate.

"Are you trying to seduce me?" I helped myself to a bite.

He flashed me a panty-melting smile. "Is it working?"

"Oh yeah."

Volkov ditched the tie and unbuttoned his collar, watching me with enough heat in his eyes to rival the pickled jalapeño I dangled from my pinky. I made a show of eating that pepper.

He groaned. "I've never been so jealous of a pickled vegetable in my life."

I laughed, then swiped a prime piece of brisket from my sandwich and brought it to his lips. He caught my wrist, his thumb stroking my arm as he bit into my offering. Instead of letting go, he kissed the inside of my wrist. Between the friction of his stubbled jaw against my skin and the wicked promise of those sinful lips, I skipped the potato salad and climbed onto his lap, wrapping my legs around his hips.

Volkov rested one hand on the curve of my back and used the other to gather my hair at the base of my neck. He kept a firm grip on my hair, using it to angle my head to the side, so he could tease my pulse with his lips.

"Hmmm. This feels familiar," I whispered. We'd been here before—at our beginning. In fact, we'd been in almost this exact position. Back then, I'd been terrified to trust another with my safety. With my heart. That first time our chemistry boiled over, I'd purposely been crude when I'd dared him to fuck me like he meant it.

Tonight, I planned to take my own advice.

Volkov let go of my hair to skim his hands up my back, dragging my t-shirt up as he went. "I seem to remember you wearing a lot fewer clothes then." Not waiting for me to ditch them, he lifted the shirt over my head and tossed it to the floor. Then, he slid the straps of my bra off my shoulders, the slow glide of the fabric as he pulled it down a tease of its own.

When I was topless, I returned the favor, unbuttoning his

crisp white dress shirt. His eyes heated as I slid the shirt from his broad shoulders and down the biceps straining the sleeves. I erased the distance between us, the press of his skin warm against my bare breasts. "If this is our last night, I want it to count."

Volkov's lips found mine for a sweet kiss.

I pulled back with a laugh, reaching in my jean pocket for a stick of gum. "I probably taste like barbecue sauce."

He took the gum from my fingers and tossed it over his shoulder with a growl. "You taste like sunshine after the rain."

Volkov captured my lips with his again, kissing me with the fierceness of a mate who would do anything in his power to ensure we had hundreds of nights just like this one. When we finally broke apart, I unwound from his body and stood on shaky legs. He widened his thighs, making room for me.

"I love you," I said softly.

"Then stay with me," he begged. "Don't make yourself a martyr tomorrow."

We both knew how fragile vessels could be. Because I couldn't promise him that, I showed him how much I loved him.

As my lips trailed across his jaw, he breathed in my scent. With my hands braced on his broad shoulders, I leaned in and dropped soft kisses to the column of his throat where he'd sported a poison ivy rash on our first date. A date he must have planned for weeks to get perfect.

I nipped the spot on his shoulder where he'd taken a silver bullet meant for me and then soothed the skin with the tip of my tongue. I'd been so terrified the silver would spread like poison until it stole him from me before we even had a chance.

Threading fingers that could tease music from ivory keys

through my hair, Volkov groaned as I worked my way down his body to trace the ridges of his abs with my tongue. I smiled at the hazy memory of bouncing on his stomach when he tried to manhandle me at Grinders. I'd been in my goat form, drunk on cheap booze and over-priced coffee beans, and I'd exposed my secret that alpha commands held no power over me.

I held Volkov's gaze as I pressed another kiss to his palm, the same hand that had turned to claw to take out men who had hurt me. First, Tony. Then, Owen Hughes and his lackey.

"Riley." He whispered my name like a prayer as his hands found my hips.

The first time we'd come together in this kitchen, I'd lied to myself that he could be a one-night stand. But from the moment we met, we were inevitable.

This time, I embraced it all—the gentle way he stroked his thumbs against my skin, the hard press of his erection against my belly when we kissed, the fierce possessiveness in his gaze as he curled a hand around the back of my neck and pulled me to him. That combination of hard man and velvet lips spiked my desire like nothing else could.

When I nipped his index finger with my teeth, his breath quickened. And when I swirled my tongue around it and sucked the finger into my warm mouth, his control snapped. Watching this man come undone was the best dessert. Volkov lifted me effortlessly, waiting until I'd wrapped my legs around him.

"No kitchen counter, tonight?" I teased, thinking about the way he'd laid me out on it like a feast our first time together. We locked eyes.

Fire and ice, Volkov's gaze flashed from amber to arctic blue. Both man and wolf focused entirely on me. "No.

Tonight, I'm going to worship this body like it deserves. Then, I'm going to remind you where you belong."

He carried me to the bedroom. "In my arms."

My back hit the mattress with a bounce.

"In my bed," he said.

I'd already divested him of his shirt, but now I watched as he kicked off his shoes and stripped off his pants. With moonlight filtering through the tall windows, I had a stellar view of his powerful body. I propped myself up on my elbows. He let me look my fill, a self-satisfied smile on his lips as my gaze tracked the hands that slowly peeled off his black boxers, his muscles flexing as he stepped free.

I crooked my finger, and he joined me on the bed.

He loomed over me. "And in my life."

Volkov teased my breasts and belly without mercy. When he moved on to flick open the button of my jeans, he lowered my zipper with excruciating slowness. I dropped my head to the mattress with a groan, my eyes drifting shut as he peeled them off me. The scrape of his stubbled jaw made my thighs tremble and the sharp sting of his teeth on my hip inspired a moan.

"Eyes on me," he ordered.

My instant compliance was rewarded when he sprawled one big hand across my stomach while the other gripped my thigh to hold me still for his tongue and teeth. No matter how much I squirmed, he didn't release his hold.

When I shattered, it was with his name on my lips and his scent on my skin.

Volkov lifted my hips, propping a pillow beneath me. His gaze locked with mine before he drove into my body with one hard thrust. But instead of giving me the tempo I begged for, he brushed my hair off my shoulder and leaned forward, fusing our bodies together. I bucked my hips, but he refused to be rushed.

With a predatory smile, he pushed up enough to blaze a trail with his lips across my neck. He paused to tease the hollow of my throat before moving that talented mouth to the shell of my ear, whispering promises I knew he'd keep. "I will slaughter a legion of demons to keep you by my side," he swore.

I cradled his face in my palms and made my own promise. "In this life and the next, I will always fight my way back to you."

With a growl building in his chest, he steadied my hips and thrust into me again and again with the wildness I craved. I arched to urge him deeper and fisted his expensive silk sheets as he obliged. Every snap of his hips reminded me I was his, and his roar as we came together, a warning to anyone who dared try to take me from him.

$\mathcal{W}$e were far more likely to stop a demon invasion than prevent small-town neighbors from nosing into our business. Nothing happened in a place as tiny as Stull, Kansas, without everyone knowing about it.

So, instead of attempting to get to the cemetery unnoticed, Volkov canvassed the town the day before to have everyone sign non-disclosures. Of course, non-disclosures weren't worth the paper they were printed on, so the Enclave also arranged for a vampire team of Shadows to wipe the memories of the entire town when this was over. Shockingly, they'd even rubber stamped the human exposure given the end-of-the-world stakes.

Several people sat in lawn chairs across the highway, with packed coolers and sparklers ready for the show. A couple of people waved to Nash as we piled out of the lineup of SUVs parked along the road in front of the cemetery. Nash raised a finger and tipped his chin like a true Midwesterner before jogging off to scout the area. His next-door neighbor Eddie rushed over with homemade chicken treats for Garth. The rooster nuzzled the old man's palm with his cheek, while Eddie praised him as a fierce fighter. Although Volkov dropped the bomb that supernaturals existed—no one in town seemed surprised—he kept Garth's alter-ego under wraps. Even in a town rumored to hold the gateway to hell, some things were better kept to ourselves.

Helen cultivated favors like a mob boss, which is how she managed to get the highway blocked off in both directions. Even with that precaution, Janis worked to erect silence and barrier wards. Because it took a lot of power to create wards on that scale, she used stones spaced evenly around the perimeter to ground and amplify the magic.

Everyone else moved into position and prepared as best we could.

I checked my watch and the sky. We still had twenty minutes until the blood moon began. The demon prophecy wasn't specific about the exact time that the vampires would attempt to open the veil, but our best guess was the moment totality began when the sun, earth, and moon would be aligned. Best-case scenario, we'd prevent the vampires from ripping the veil. Second best would be to seal it as soon as it opened. Legions of demons could come through in the span of an hour—the time frame expected for tonight's blood moon. And that wasn't even the worst-case scenario because the prophecy didn't specify whether the veil would remain open indefinitely or be limited to the lunar eclipse.

Volkov posted sentries at regular intervals within a half-a-mile radius, and everyone was equipped with comms so anyone could raise the warning at the first sighting of vampires descending upon the cemetery. Most of us congregated near the Stull Cemetery gates. Despite the stakes, it felt wrong to trample the graves of the people laid to rest here.

With twenty minutes to go, I checked to make sure everyone was here and ready. When we recruited the representatives for each breed born of earth, we aimed for the strongest among each faction. As the necromancer, Kali positioned herself close to me. Volkov shifted into his massive black wolf and guarded my other side with amber eyes that promised death to any demon who ventured too close. Between the girls, it was a toss-up who was the strongest, but Bea filled the witch role tonight. And although Dez might not be the strongest vampire, he was the only one I'd trust to have my back.

The human representative was the trickiest opening to fill. Unless we wanted Eddie or one of his neighbors to step in, which seemed like a disaster waiting to happen, we were stuck with Nash filling two roles tonight—human representative and one of the five guardians.

Along with Nash, we had Helen, Craig, Sato, and Garth to round out our guardians. Helen stood in the center of a warded circle on one side of the cemetery gate, a fanny pack full of potion bombs and a demon banishing spell ready to use on any dumb enough to step into the giant salt circle next to hers. Garth stalked around her, his beady red eyes glowing in the dark.

Nash crouched on the other side of the gate in another warded circle with an arsenal of weapons within reach, the most important of which was a war scythe honed in hellfire and capable of killing demons. The rest of the demon weapons Sato brought had been distributed among Volkov's shifters. I rolled my eyes at the canteen next to his grenade launcher, certain he'd filled it with holy water despite my insistence it wouldn't do jack to a demon.

Craig stood next to Kali, capable of fighting on land or air. And because Nate Irons took his vow to guard Sierra seriously, he hovered nearby. With two hulking gargoyles able to turn to stone, they might offer us enough protection to combine and use our magic. Hopefully, bulletproof translated to hellfire.

Shortly after we arrived, Sato shifted into his massive beast. He wasn't anything like I'd expected. Rather than the bulky fire-breathing dragons of fairy tales, Kage Sato was sleek like a snake and fanged like a vampire, his long, scaled body undulating as he rode the breeze like a wave to guard the cemetery from the air. He turned his head my way as if sensing my attention and breathed out a stream of water that turned to vapor as I watched. I might not like Sato, but that didn't stop me from watching him in awe. No wonder Volkov couldn't intimidate him.

The elementals who'd be funneling me their power surrounded me. Normally, elemental powers didn't manifest until late adolescence, but at twelve, Sierra was already the strongest wielder of not just one, but two elements—water and air. I'd given her another chance to bow out of this fight before we headed over here, but she'd chosen to stand at my side. We didn't have enough time to find a true earth elemental, so Janis and Alyce were both lending their magic to fill that role.

That left fire. While the others risked being tapped out when I drew their magic into my body, as our fire elemental, Liv risked the most. According to Sato, ordinary fire wouldn't be strong enough to power the seal, so she would need to wield hellfire drawn from my dagger and add it to the mix.

"Are you sure?" I asked her as she petted my blade like a weirdo. Liv seemed to love weapons the way I loved barbecue. "We have no idea if a witch can even withstand hellfire. Regardless of what Sato says, we can try with normal fire." After the stunt he pulled at the airport, I didn't trust his judgement, anyway.

Liv rolled her shoulders and grinned. "Oh yeah. I'm sure. The last few weeks have been so boring." She kissed the hilt of my dagger. "This is gonna be epic."

"That's the spirit." With everyone in position, I reached for Sierra's hand. "You ready?"

Sierra set her shoulders and braced her legs like a fighter. "I was born a weapon." There was no pride in her statement, only resigned acceptance.

"No. You're a warrior. There's a difference." At her nod, I offered Sierra a stick of gum. "Here. This will help with the nerves."

The longer we stood here without the vamps showing up, the more uneasy I felt. There was no time to second-guess our location though, so I shook out a second piece of gum and shoved it into my mouth, the warm bite of cinnamon settling my own nerves. "Ten minutes and counting," I said into the comms. "Everyone ready?"

The chorus of yeses was immediate. We were as ready as we would ever be. Now, all we could do was wait and hope we'd guessed right.

"Okay girls, bring it in." Bea herded all the elementals into a group huddle, the scent of her hairspray as comforting as my gum. "Alright everyone, this is it." She fluffed her bottle-blonde hair and tugged the plunging neckline of her leopard-print shirt a bit lower. "Time to bring that big titty energy."

Alyce, Janis, and Liv nodded. Sierra clamped a hand over

her mouth to hold in her giggle. Volkov swung his massive black head our way with a huff. I stared pointedly at my modest assets and raised a brow.

Bea clapped me on the back. "Don't fret, sugar. It's an attitude, not a cup size." She glanced around our circle. "Now, let's go kick some demon ass."

CHAPTER 31

*E*veryone was so focused on intercepting vampires that no one noticed the witch infiltrating our group. Zara Bellarose joined the party disguised as one of Volkov's wolves, dropping the illusion when she was within striking distance.

"Girls," she greeted Sierra and me.

Volkov's hackles rose, and he bared his teeth, putting himself between us. Alpha Irons moved closer to Sierra, ready to tear Bellarose apart with his bare hands.

"Kind of busy here," I snapped. "We don't have time for your games, Bellarose. And none of us are letting you sacrifice Sierra."

Bellarose ignored the snarling werewolf and terrifying gargoyle to tssk at me. "Riley dear, that was never the plan. Sierra was made to stop the demons just as you were." Her smile was patronizing and her dark eyes victorious as she held her arms out wide. "This is your destiny."

"If you didn't intend to sacrifice Sierra, then why were you about to auction her to the vamps?" I kept Sierra's hand tucked into mine, letting her know she wasn't facing this evil woman alone.

Bellarose had the audacity to look offended. "That auction would've drawn the vamps out, so I could slaughter them like cattle." She shook her head. "When the vamps open the veil, it'll be because you screwed up the plan."

A sick feeling grew in the pit of my stomach because I didn't think she was lying. "Even if that was your plan, you used Sierra as bait, and worse, you convinced her that her only value was as a weapon."

Sierra flinched but didn't pull her hand from mine.

"She is a weapon, just as you are the vessel." Bellarose's dark eyes held a hint of madness. "Sierra has been trained since birth to fulfill her purpose as you should have been. The Seers foretold this when I was still a child. And I did what had to be done. Sometimes, sacrifices must be made to serve the greater good."

The idea that Sierra lost her childhood made me sick. No wonder she locked her emotions down tight. She must've been pushed relentlessly to develop her powers long before she even understood what those powers meant. If it weren't for Amelia and Santiago, that would've been my fate as well.

"Why is it," I gritted out between clenched teeth, "that the people who love to preach sacrifice are never the ones willing to make it?"

Bellarose cocked her head to the side and stared at me. "What greater sacrifice could there be than my daughters?"

I swayed on my feet as her words dug in like claws. "Sierra is your daughter." I locked eyes with the girl still clinging to my hand like a lifeline. "My sister." I had a sister. The horror of what Bellarose stole from us sank in.

Between the lack of vampires at the cemetery and the

revelation hanging in the air, I missed the moment the Earth slid between the sun and moon. The corresponding rip in the veil happened so fast, all we could do was react. We'd been so certain that vampires would tear the veil from our side that it never occurred to us that the demons might break through from theirs.

Unlike us, the demons had millennia to prepare for this invasion, and it showed. They moved with military precision through the opening, fanning out as they came through. No amount of illustrations could prepare me for the terror they struck as they descended like a swarm upon us. Their massive forms dwarfed our fighters on the ground—huge, grotesque bodies with horns and claws.

We couldn't worry about the demons that made it through —not until we sealed the realms. Our guardians and fighters formed a shield around us, with Sato engaging the airborne demons with water and ice, while Volkov and the others kept the demons on the ground from reaching the magic wielders.

I shoved aside my shock and fear, ignored the betrayal, and launched into action because there were only two sides in this war. "Now," I shouted.

Zara Bellarose threw off her cloak and raised her arms to the sky, the blood runes painted on her skin glowing red like the moon overhead. Her hands and lips moved to cast illu sions that shimmered to life. Doppelgangers so good that without the glow of magic around them, I wouldn't have been able to distinguish them from my friends.

Sierra, Alyce, and Janis called their elements to them, the energy from so much magic thick in the air. I opened myself to it, breathing slow and deep like Santiago taught me as I drew the magic into my lungs, stored it deep in my belly, and came back for more. I blocked out the fighting all around me.

Trusting my mate to keep the enemy at bay, I soaked up the elements like a sponge until the combined magic danced and crackled beneath my skin. When I shook with the effort to contain it, I yelled for Liv to feed me hellfire.

Liv busted the stone on my dagger and called forth the hellfire, her hair lighting up with flames as she battled to withstand its heat. I reached for her fire, and the heat of it burned me from the inside out until tears poured down my cheeks and my mouth locked in a silent scream. My arms shook from the elements bottled up inside me until I was afraid I'd burst. And still I waited, pulled more power until I couldn't draw any more. Using my mother's ring on my left hand to ground me, I channeled all the elemental magic inside me into the signet ring on my right hand. When I was drained of magic, I waited for the runes to light up.

Nothing happened.

"Again," I shouted. But no matter how many times I channeled their magic, it wasn't enough. Then, the answer came.

Five breeds. Five guardians. Five elements.

I needed the fifth element to make this work. "Kali, I need you to draw spirit magic. Add it to the mix."

Kali didn't hesitate. She dropped her shields and drew power from the hollowed ground. And this time when I pulled from the elements, the runes on the signet ring lit up. But the veil didn't seal.

A scaled dragon rode the wind to the ground, changing into Kage Sato as he touched down. He strode toward us, pausing to throw up a wall of ice to block the demon that attacked him. "The veil can only be sealed from the side that opened it," he called and then launched himself into the sky.

"No one can withstand walking through hellfire and live to seal it," I whispered.

"Maybe with Raum, I could do it," Kali offered.

Craig had her wrapped in stone arms before she could take a step in that direction.

"No," both Craig and I shouted at once.

"Let me take it," Dez offered, his earnest eyes glazed with bloodlust from the fight. "Let me save you the way you saved me."

I grabbed his arm and shook my head. "No way, Dez."

Before anyone else could offer, Liv swiped the signet ring off my finger. "Dibs," she yelled, sprinting for the rip in the veil with the ring in her hand. "Be right back."

I might not be able to wade into the flames myself, but that didn't mean I had to stand here and do nothing. Sierra's slight body trembled with exhaustion, her control over the elements weakened. But I could help her. "Sierra, are you tapped out, or can you feed me more power?"

Her slight body trembled with exhaustion, but she did it anyway, giving me the fuel I needed to blast the demons coming through the veil. It didn't stop them, but it gave Liv a distraction. Unfortunately, no amount of water put out hellfire. I tried, anyway.

When she got close, Liv slid like a baseball player stealing a base, her body skidding past the demons marching out of hell. The ring slipped from her grip as she rolled to the side just in time to escape being trampled under the oncoming demons' feet, stopping inches from the opening. She staggered to her knees and fumbled for the ring, but one of the demons plucked her from the ground and tossed her into the flames.

I lunged in her direction, but Volkov cut me off with a snarl. Nate Irons beat me to the rescue, charging through the horde. He reached through the veil and grabbed Liv, hauling her out with a scream I felt in my bones. When he pulled his arm from the flames, the stone turned to ash everywhere the hellfire had touched. For a second, he froze, staring down where his hand should be. The demons descended from all sides, and he had no choice but to fight his way free.

Before anyone else could go for that ring, Garth dove into the fray. He turned around when he reached it and crowed loud enough to cut through the din of battle, locking eyes with Helen for a heartbeat. Garth plucked the ring from the ground with his beak and darted through the veil. As soon as he cleared it, he grew ten feet tall with razor sharp horns and a battle roar. The rip sealed as fast as it opened, leaving the rest of us safe on this side and Garth trapped in hell.

CHAPTER 32

*S*ix *Months Later*

The last months had been a rollercoaster, but we were all alive thanks to Garth's sacrifice. And Nate Iron's decisive action. Sadly, there was no regenerating a hand lost to hellfire, but the girls gave him the next best thing, a state-of-the-art prosthetic infused with magic that allowed it to shift when he did.

Nash wouldn't admit how much he missed our feathered menace, but he came home a few weeks ago with a cardboard box full of baby chicks and enough lumber to build a coop. Helen took Garth's loss the hardest until she discovered the Ouija board he left behind worked like a telephone in a summoning circle. We now had a weekly conference call to hell in conjunction with coven game night.

She bragged about him to anyone who would listen since her insistence he had leadership potential proved true. Because Garth had been the one to seal the veil, he'd claimed the high crown, reigning supreme over all the demons remaining in hell. The demons who slipped through the veil before Garth sealed it and escaped hadn't been found yet. But that was a problem for another day.

Right now, we all stood in front of headquarters. Everyone gazed up at the new and improved sign Bennie had made. Nash installed it for me above the big bay door yesterday. I was happy to see the two of them bonding over wood-working.

Volkov wrapped an arm around my waist and brushed a kiss against my temple. "You sure you're ready to give up high-stakes heists?"

"For now, at least." Necessity had made me a great thief, but there were a lot of ways to get an adrenaline fix and, for the first time, I had the freedom to explore all of them. Even without Volkov's resources, I'd stashed away most of my last paycheck, which was more than enough to fund an extended sabbatical. "What do you think?" I asked the group.

Sierra nodded solemnly. "It's perfect."

At first, the Enclave made a stink about Sierra living with us full time, but Helen and I threatened to expose every bit of dirt we'd dug up on them if they tried to take her. Destroying a corrupt power structure could go two ways—one that ended in rubble and one that tore it down brick by brick. As long as they left us alone, we were content to keep dismantling it one brick at a time.

Volkov still worried my status as a siphon and Sierra's burgeoning powers put targets on our backs, and his response to any perceived threat to us tended to be hands on. Sierra also had a veritable supernatural army willing to battle for her. Plus, my ability to drain magic made most supernaturals wary.

Neither Sierra nor I had any contact with Zara Bellarose. Although I pitied her for the messed-up childhood Bellarose endured with a father who used his visions to convince her that her greatest calling was to birth sacrificial daughters to save the world, it didn't erase the damage she caused. Based on what we knew about the Cerberus project and the lengths Bellarose went to in order to manipulate both Sierra and me, someone on the Enclave had to be working with her, and her father was the logical guess. Not that I could prove it. Serving on the Enclave required abandoning their former lives though, and his mysterious disappearance fit. I tamped down all thoughts of Bellarose and focused on the women who showed up today to support my new venture.

Helen and the girls admired our new sign. It still spelled out G.O.A.T. in big neon letters, but below it, we'd reinterpreted the acronym. It now read Guild of Adventurous Teens. It'd taken a lot of brainstorming to settle on guild, but Dez convinced me that dubbing headquarters open to gangs of adventurous teens was a terrible idea. He had a point.

I offered Sierra our pair of giant scissors and motioned to the big pink ribbon stretched across the front of the building. "You wanna do the honors?"

She hesitated, as if afraid she'd mess it up. I waited until she made up her mind, handing over the scissors when she reached for them. She cut through the ribbon as the rest of us cheered. Although we were calling this a christening, the only people here to celebrate were friends and family. Soon enough, I'd open these doors to the public.

Everyone spent the next hour huddled over game tables and the snack bar as I told them all about the center for at-risk supernatural teens I was opening here. What I lacked in formal degrees and adolescent program development experience, I'd make up for in enthusiasm. Sierra and I had spent the last months getting to know each other and imagining a center where kids who were on the fringes of supernatural society could have a safe place where they could figure out for themselves who they were and what kind of future they wanted. We'd dreamed up obstacle courses with plenty of climbing, recreation classes led by our witches, and a library brimming with magic and beanbags to provide hours of escape.

As we finished telling the group about our big plans, Sierra beamed at me. Her smiles were still rare, but I treasured every one like a gift. I played it cool though, not wanting to risk making her feel self-conscious. But when my eyes met Volkov's across the room, I saw the same fierce joy in those whiskey depths that beat inside my chest. His wolf receded, and the man smiled at me.

Bea nudged my hip. "You girls ready for your big makeover?"

I grinned, peeking inside the bag she carried. She'd thought of everything from hair dye to sparkly eyeshadow. Bea held open the bag so Sierra could see inside. "What do you think, Sierra? It's not too late to change your mind."

Sierra tipped her chin. "Not a chance."

Volkov gave me a kiss hot enough that Bea catcalled and Sierra gagged. By the time he pulled away, I was considering forgoing the makeover to sneak off with him.

"Nuh uh," Bea wrapped a hand around my bicep and propelled me toward the bathroom. "There'll be plenty of time to get naked later."

Sierra covered her ears. "Gross!"

I laughed.

Bea made a shooing motion to Volkov. "Go on. You can pick us up at seven. That should give us plenty of time to set up."

He raised a brow but didn't argue. Everyone else followed him out, promising to meet us at the venue later tonight.

Kali hovered at the door. "I'll be back in a couple hours with some outfits. I need to pick up Junior from Magic Paws. He's been out of sorts since Garth left."

A pang of sadness hit. I missed Garth, too. A seance wasn't the same as having him here.

Kali let herself out, and Bea got to work. "Who wants to go first?" she asked.

Sierra clutched the box of hair dye to her chest. "Me!"

An hour and a half later, Sierra gazed at her bright teal hair in the bathroom mirror. The color transformed her. She laughed and spun in a circle before leaning close to the mirror again to admire the colorful shoulder-length bob. Then, she threw her arms around Bea and hugged her. While Bea and I both choked up, Sierra raced to her new bedroom to change her clothes for tonight's main event.

Volkov returned at seven on the dot, dressed in blue jeans and a dark blue t-shirt that highlighted his sculpted chest. Sierra intercepted him at the door, and he declared his love for her bright new hairstyle. When he finally looked up and caught sight of me, he stared. "You changed your hair."

"It was time." For ten years, I'd needed the armor my pink hair provided. It allowed me to reinvent myself, choose to be seen, but it had also been a way to deny the girl I'd been. And that girl was a survivor. I was finally ready to embrace both versions of me, so I'd asked Bea to dye my hair back to its original dark blonde. I'd kept a streak of pink in the front though. "What do you think?"

"I think I'm the luckiest man in the world." Volkov hauled me close and kissed me until Sierra tossed a pillow at our heads.

"Save it for the after party." She grabbed both our hands and urged us toward the door.

Volkov dug in his heels. "Not so fast. I have something for you first." He reached into his pocket and brought out a small velvet bag, shaking the necklace loose. "This belonged to my sister Anya." Volkov flicked the locket open and showed Sierra the childhood picture of him and his sister. They both looked so happy and carefree. He closed it with a smile and held it out to Sierra. "She would've wanted you to have it."

Sierra froze. She stared down at the delicate gold locket Volkov held out to her. "What if I lose it?" she whispered.

"You won't." He spoke with the confidence of an alpha.

It worked. She turned around and lifted her hair so he could fasten it around her neck. She ran a finger over the engraved heart. "I've never had jewelry before."

I swallowed past the lump in my throat at the idea of her missing out on so many things. All I could do is fill her future with enough experiences to make up for it. The three of us piled into Volkov's Audi, both Sierra and I immediately cranking up the toasty heated seats. I turned on the radio, and we all sang along to pop songs on the drive to Kauffman Theatre.

When we arrived, the guys already had everything set up for the show. We joined them on stage for a sound check. Nash tuned his guitar. Not even Sierra could convince Nash to ditch his acoustic guitar for an electric one. After months of practice, Dez was getting pretty good on drums. Sierra gasped when she spotted the new keyboard that we'd special ordered for this event.

Volkov nudged her toward it. "Go check it out." He stiffened when he caught sight of the two stunning women making their way to the front row. "I'm going to kill my mother. Why the fuck would she bring her here?"

I waved. "I invited Nadia. We're taking Sierra thrifting tomorrow." Irina and I were still finding our footing, but Nadia and I had six months' worth of chat history bonding us. When she said she'd be in Chicago, I talked her into joining Irina for a visit.

"Of course, you did." Volkov reeled me in for a kiss, then spun me toward the rest of the band, and slapped my denim-clad butt. "Go bring down the house."

Liv bounced on stage, waving for me to join her on the mic. Even from here, I could see the flash of the knife strapped to her thigh. I spun around for one more good luck kiss before I joined her at the mic. Unlike me, Liv could carry a tune. Not that I'd let it stop me.

She whistled. "Love the hair, girls."

I primped and warmed up my vocal chords as I watched the stadium fill up. Everyone came out for our very first rock concert. Volkov's whole pack turned out, along with our coven decked out in raunchy rock-n-roll t-shirts, Kali and Craig, and even half of the Kansas City Coven of the Divine Sisterhood of Sacred Truth showed up. I had no idea who half of the rest of these people were, but knowing Volkov, he'd probably strong-armed everyone he knew into coming.

"You ready?" I asked everyone.

Nash and Liv both gave me a thumbs up.

But Dez had completely zoned out, staring at the woman talking with Volkov in the front row. With long, sable hair and a curvy figure, she was gorgeous. Add the hot librarian glasses and bulky cable-knit sweater, and Dez wasn't the only one staring at her.

I snapped my finger to get his attention. "Dez!"

He stumbled and crashed into the drum set, turning bright red when she looked his way, giving him a little finger wave and a smirk. "Who is that?" he breathed, practically drooling.

Oh, this was too good. I laughed. "Dez, that's Arlo."

Instead of launching into his normal competitive diatribe, he leaned on the drum set, causing another racket. "I think I'm in love."

Nash snorted.

Once Dez managed to pry his gaze from the raccoon shifter he was now in love with, I checked to make sure Sierra was ready for her very first concert. She stood frozen behind the keyboard, all the blood drained from her face as she stared out at the growing crowd. "Oh shit."

Before I could come up with a pep talk, Volkov had noticed and vaulted onto the stage. "Hey, you've got this, sweetheart," he assured.

She grasped his t-shirt and looked at him with terror. "But they're all watching me. What if I mess up?" Her dark eyes brimmed with tears.

Volkov ran his hand across his neck and blew out a breath. He moved behind the keyboard next to her. "What if we do this together?"

Sierra nodded slowly. "Okay."

The lights dimmed and the audience quieted, the first notes of the keyboard one more memory we were making. For the rest of the night, I belted out my favorite rock songs like I owned this stage.

Thank you for reading *Graveside Gambler*. For a sneak peek

into Liv's series, sign up to my newsletter to get her prequel, *Inferno Bound.*

NEWSLETTER SIGNUP

Subscribe to my newsletter for updates, announcements, contests, and bonus content: lamcbride.com/newsletter/

NOTE TO READERS

If you enjoyed this book, please consider leaving a review or rating on Amazon and/or Goodreads. Your reviews help new readers discover my books and are always appreciated!

If you'd like to be notified of new releases and exclusive content, you can sign up for my newsletter at lamcbride.com/newsletter/ and join my Facebook Readers Group at https://www.facebook.com/groups/lamcbridereaders

ALSO BY L.A. MCBRIDE

Each series can be read independently, but they are set in the same world with some character crossover.

KALI JAMES SERIES

Book 1: Fastening the Grave

Book 2: Threading the Bones

Book 3: Stitching the Talisman

Book 4: Gathering the Dead

RILEY CRUZ SERIES

Prequel: Boneyard Thief

Book 1: Relic Hunter

Book 2: Brimstone Burglar

Book 3: Magic Heist

Book 4: Cursed Vault

Book 5: Graveside Gambler

ACKNOWLEDGMENTS

Thank you to my amazing beta readers Krista and Stephanie, who dropped everything to read chapters for me, and to my husband Chris who is my first reader and my greatest support. I'm so grateful for my assistant Jordan and my amazing ARC team for reading my books, catching typos, and spreading the Riley love. The biggest thank you goes to my readers, who patiently wait for my stories. Your support means the world.

Printed in Dunstable, United Kingdom

69130530R00143